CARDBOARD IN MY BOOTS

BY

LESLEY JEFFERIES

Copyright © Lesley Jefferies 2017
This book is sold subject to the condition that it shall not, by way of trade or otherwise, be lent, resold, hired out, or otherwise circulated without the publisher's prior consent in any form of binding or cover other than that in which it is published and without a similar condition including this condition being imposed on the subsequent publisher.
The moral right of Lesley Jefferies has been asserted.
ISBN-13: 978-1541105751
ISBN-10: 1541105753

This book is dedicated to my husband, who, without his patience the book would never have been written, and also to my cocker spaniel who kept me company in the office for hours at a time.

CONTENTS

Chapter 1 .... *1*
Chapter 2 .... *6*
Chapter 3 .... *14*
Chapter 4 .... *20*
Chapter 5 .... *24*
Chapter 6 .... *28*
Chapter 7 .... *32*
Chapter 8 .... *40*
Chapter 9 .... *52*
Chapter 10 .... *64*
Chapter 11 .... *69*
Chapter 12 .... *72*
Chapter 13 .... *85*
Chapter 14 .... *93*
Chapter 15 .... *104*
Chapter 16 .... *113*
Chapter 17 .... *116*
Chapter 18 .... *122*
Chapter 19 .... *133*
Chapter 20 .... *136*
Chapter 21 .... *146*
Chapter 22 .... *151*
Chapter 23 .... *165*
Chapter 24 .... *175*
Chapter 25 .... *180*
Chapter 26 .... *185*
Chapter 27 .... *189*
Chapter 28 .... *194*

Chapter 29	200
Chapter 30	207
Chapter 31	211
Chapter 32	218
Chapter 33	223
Chapter 34	230
Chapter 35	237
Chapter 36	241
Chapter 37	246
Chapter 38	251
Chapter 39	258
Chapter 40	261
Chapter 41	267
Chapter 42	273
Chapter 43	276
Chapter 44	278

Although this book is a work of fiction it is taken from true childhood memories. Names, characters, businesses, places, events and incidents are either the products of the author's imagination or used in a fictitious manner. Any resemblance to actual persons, living or dead, or actual events is purely coincidental.

Chapter 1

The sun was rising slowly over the streets of London, bathing it with its first rays of light and rinsing it with a gentle warmth, taking away the dark shadows and hidden secrets as it hit the dust-covered rubble. Bouncing off the scattered remains of the houses, revealing the devastation caused from the nocturnal bombing expedition. Pressing my nose against the glass, it looked like a sprinkle of snow had covered the ground and as my eyes became accustomed to the light I could see as far as the observatory in Greenwich Park. Looking over my shoulder, my elder brother Sid was still asleep. He had thrown the covers off the bed in the night and his long gangly leg was hanging over the side, revealing a large foot with a dirty grey striped sock hanging off the end. He was snoring loudly and the noise was quite deafening as it echoed round the nearly empty room. I was cold from the lack of heating, my breath like puffs of smoke hit the window, immediately freezing and until I rubbed it with my sleeve, blocked my view. I pulled my very old grey woollen dressing gown around me to try and gain some additional warmth from the ancient garment, which, yet again had been another hand-me-down, having once belonged to Dad. It was at least three sizes too big for me and I was constantly falling over the hem, much to Sid's amusement.

With all the wheezing and grunting that was coming from the bed, I was awake before the rest of the household. Sharing a bed with Sid was quite an act of tolerance, but the only other spare room had been delegated to my younger sister Sally. I must say I would have rather shared with her, and I thought it unfair that just because she was a girl she was entitled to have her own room. But me mum made the rules and we had to keep to them on fear of death. She had very strict demands and if we strayed far from her principles we would have to answer to her anger, which could mean anything from doing the weekly shopping, cleaning the house, or even scrubbing out the outside toilet. Sid always managed to avoid these chores, and it always seemed to be me caught with the bucket and mop in my hand. Sid was a tall lad for thirteen, with black greasy hair which he hardly ever washed. He was forever brushing his fringe off his forehead, keeping it long so that it would cover his increasing number of yellow boils that appeared overnight. He had the first signs of stubble appearing on his chin, of which extremely proud, he constantly brought attention to it by refusing to shave.

He never was one for the girls, though. They seemed to dislike him due to his disagreeable personality. Nearly every night I would be tossed from the bed due to his wild thrashings and I would have to spend the night on the old wooden floor with just a single sheet to cover me and a cushion off the downstairs sofa for a pillow. In the winter mornings I would wake frozen, my skin would have a bluish tinge, my fingers stiff, my lips would be stuck together and I could not bend my toes until I jumped up and down for at least ten minutes. I was always frightened that certain parts of my anatomy had dropped off in the night. Well Sid tried to frighten me into thinking this, but Mum told me not to believe a word he said. But in the morning I would reach down to make sure everything was still there.

Sid was a few years older and towered above me in height. I was nine when we moved to the terraced house in Blackheath. Small for my age, nearly having died after contracting scarlet fever when I was younger, I was a little slower growing than other boys of a similar age. Sid, however, never stood in my corner, encouraging the boys in our street to take the mickey. If it had not been for my sister Sally, who always stood up to them, putting her fists up trying to protect me, I would have taken a lot more stick. Although none of them were willing to fight a girl and always walked away from her; though she was small as a person you'd never want to pick a quarrel with her.

The attic where we slept had sloping ceilings and Sid and I often hit our heads when climbing from the creaky wrought iron bed. Sometimes when Sid got up in the night and went to the bathroom I would hear a loud thud and hear him curse and swear as he walked down the corridor. Some I'd never heard before. In the morning, I'd ask me mum what they meant. But all I got from her was a sharp clip around the ear, and was told not to repeat such rude language. Mum would then say, "If only your father were still around, Bob. He'd strike you down, son, if he could hear you say that."

Me dad, that was another story altogether. Bert, as he was called, met me mum, Connie, who had just turned twenty, at the Ally Pally. She was quite a looker in her time. Slim shapely legs, peroxide short, blonde, curled hair, full pursed heart-shaped lips and long red nails. Dad used to say they could scratch a man's back into sheer ecstasy. He'd approached Mum for a dance. She had said no at first, because she had her eye on another bloke that night, and he was a young pilot, who, in his uniform was causing a bit of a stir. However, by the end of the night, she realised he was more interested in her friend Phyllis who had made sure she'd danced with him all evening. Bert made one final attempt to ask her to dance. He would have given up if she'd said no that time. There was only so much rejection a bloke could put up with. Realising she had no other choice as everyone else seemed to have taken to the dance floor already, she agreed to a jive. That one dance changed her mind about him. He didn't seem to be that bad. Perhaps she'd copped the best bloke after all. She'd thought it at the time anyhow. Mum used to love to tell us how they met and told the story time and again. We missed having Dad around for a long time after he went. That was the start of Sid's bad behaviour.

Mum just lost control.

Chapter 2

Bert was a polite and well-liked man. He was not particularly good looking but tall and slim and in his navy blue pinstriped suit and wearing his glasses, he looked remarkably intelligent. Nothing like the cockney car salesman that he was. He was very serious and didn't laugh much. He was different from all the other lads Connie met. Bert talked very fast, like he was nervous. Mum learnt afterwards, he always did. It was because he was born a salesman and never knew when to stop. Neither of them had realised it was so late. Connie was worried when they missed the last bus home and then had to walk the five miles to Lewisham from the Pally.

It was a fine night and as the first sign of light appeared it brought with it a gusty wind which pushed them forward as they walked. The streets were empty and eerily silent. The birds had not begun their early morning twittering. The dawn breaking looked remarkably like an orange had been squeezed and the juice spurting in all directions had sprayed the street with light, just as everything was about to erupt into its usual daily chaos. They walked faster, Bert holding her hand all the way.

Suddenly stopping, he pulled her towards him; before Connie could change her mind he grabbed a kiss, just before they reached the end of the road. Connie licked his lips almost like she was indulging in a luscious cream cake for the first time. She had never been kissed with so much force. Her knees buckled but Bert caught her, stopping her from falling. He smiled cheekily as if he had just done something he shouldn't and with a saucy wink and a strong grip supporting her, they walked towards the council flats where Connie lived. Jean, Connie's mother, was waiting outside the front entrance. She had lived there for over twelve years with her three other daughters. A single mum left by a flighty husband. Hair in curlers, arms crossed, and wearing an old pink dressing gown. Completing the look was a pair of white fluffy slippers. Bert thought they looked ridiculous and tried hard not to laugh. She had the look of a mother relieved, but who was just about to commit a murder as Connie was so late home. It was

4.30 in the morning and Connie had been out nearly all night. Bubbling with rage like a bottle that was about to go pop, Jean walked towards them. No hint of a smile could be seen on her face.

All she was lacking was the rolling pin.

"I hope you're the marrying kind," she said to Bert, taking her daughter by the arm and attempting to march her back up the three flights of stairs to their third-floor flat.

"I am," Bert said, laughing. "I'll see you at the Pally Saturday."

Connie turned round and gave him her most enticing smile in an attempt to give the impression that there was a lot more on offer if he saw her again. Trying to untangle herself from Jean's grasp she climbed the stairs, followed by her mum who never drew breath but nagged Connie all the way up to the flat, one, for letting a strange boy walk her home and two, for being so late. Connie climbed into bed next to her sister Sally, pulled the covers up under her chin, turned to her sister and said, "I've just met the man I'm going to marry." Then, kissing her sister goodnight on the cheek, tried to manoeuvre herself into a more comfortable position before she could go to sleep.

The whole household was already awake and the sound of noisy chatter and giggling could be heard. Knowing breakfast was well underway. Connie reluctantly climbed out of bed. After having only had a few hours sleep, she was still exhausted and not in the best of moods. Hurrying down the narrow corridor following the inviting smell of hot coffee that was coming from the kitchen she bumped smack, into her little sister Sylvia, who in her eagerness to squeeze past Connie tipped her drink precariously sideways, allowing some of her hot chocolate to spill over the floor. Connie dived forward and expertly caught the mug like a goalkeeper in the World Cup defending a penalty shot. Managing to save the remainder of the chocolate from splashing onto the already well stained carpet, as this seemed to happen on a daily basis. Sylvia a sweet girl, but naughty due to an unfortunate accident at birth when she had been starved of oxygen and for a few moments had stopped breathing. This sadly, was the reason for her slow development and why she appeared a little backward and sometimes very childish. The girls all loved her, protecting her fiercely from people that made unkind comments. Who ignorant of her slightly strange characteristics, although funny to the family, to outsiders would often appear rude.

"Mum says you're courting. Does that mean I can have me own bedroom soon?"

Connie laughed. "Maybe," she said. "Just maybe." She loved Sylvia but she could be so annoying sometimes. Connie returned to the bedroom to decide what she was going to wear when she next saw Bert. Closely followed by her younger sister who was proving to be more of a hindrance than a help, Connie went through her wardrobe. She wanted to look sexy but not too available. Bert should know she was a good girl, from a nice family and she just needed something to keep him interested. Nothing seemed suitable. Looking miserably at herself in the mirror after trying dress after dress and listening to Sylvia's unkind comments which had reduced her to tears and compelled her confidence to disappear as if by magic out the window. She sat down on the edge of the bed opened the bedside drawer and took out her money box , forcibly removed the rubber stopper from the little pink China Pig and shook the contents violently onto the coverlet, disappointed there was not enough to buy even a packet of fags let alone a new dress. Looking sadly at the small collection of coins scattered beside her on the bedspread and knowing she wasn't going to be paid until the following Friday she sat wondering if her mum would sub her. She didn't think so somehow. The local department store, she'd look there. They had a dress department that would have something – she'd get it on tic. Normally a trifle too expensive. A girl, however, had to do what girl had to do. Connie dressed with one eye on the clock, not wanting to miss the bus. She might just have time to look in their window. That was if the bus was on time. Quickly checking over her appearance, she grabbed her handbag, said goodbye to her little sister, gave her a quick hug and slammed the door shut. As she hurried down the steps, the sound of her high heels could be heard clip clopping loudly as the metal tips on her stiletto shoes hit the concrete. She ran past graffiti covered walls, covered in drawings of cartoon characters with abusive slogans sprayed in red paint. Opening the large glass swinging doors she stepped out into the street and immediately the unpleasant aroma of rotting food reached her nostrils. Taking a deep breath of fresh air she pulled the navy woollen hat that Jean had knitted to match her coat further down over her ears. It gave her little protection from the cold frosty morning as the winter sun on its arrival had brought no warmth to the day. Moving swiftly past the dustbins which had not been emptied and were overflowing with the remains of Friday night's fish and chips. The city foxes having helped themselves overnight to the leftovers. Leaving the empty cartons and half eaten remains of smelly fish from their evening meal scattered untidily across the pavement. Covering her face with her hanky she quickened her step until she passed the cause of the odious smell. Connie took her places at the bus stop joining the end of a very long queue and waited patiently for the Number 52 to arrive. Day dreaming of Bert. What she would wear and how much she was looking forward to seeing him again. He would be her ticket out of this awful place. And she knew by any which way she could, she was going to marry him.

Saturday arrived, Connie wore the new dress, she had spent her whole week's wages on it, desperately wanting to outshine Phyllis, who had nasty habit of stealing her boyfriends from right under her nose. The dress was from the local department store. Connie had always wanted to work there but her accounting skills had not been quite up to the standard they required. At the interview having been asked to complete a mathematical equation and failing miserably, mathematics not being her strongest attribute. Had been told at the time that unfortunately her application had been unsuccessful and for the present they were unable to offer her a position. The pink sequinned dress had been in the window all week. Connie had been unable to resist, she would have to owe the housekeeping money this week. Although she knew Jean would be furious, it just had to be done. The dress was just perfect. Pink nails, pink lips, pink dress. A vision indeed. Although as Bert muttered under his breath, "Perhaps just a little too much pink."

It was the early hours of the morning by the time Connie looked at the clock and realised how late it was. Her feet hurt and she was thirsty having only taken the occasional drink from a glass of beer which had stood nearly all night on the table untouched. So enthralled with each other's company they had not stopped talking and dancing. They couldn't believe how late it was. "Mum will be furious. We're going to be late home again. You'll have to marry me now. My reputation is compromised," Connie said, giggling.

Bert saw Connie constantly over the next few months. He failed to mention, though, that he sometimes took Phyllis for an occasional drink as well, which sometimes turned into more than just a little drink, much to Bert's eagerness to get twenty notches on his bedpost. He was making every attempt he could to beat his friend Micky at the number of times they'd done it. Micky was in the lead at the moment. Although, Bert did keep telling him that touching did not count.

Chapter 3

Connie looked at herself in the mirror, thinking front ways she didn't look too bad. Sideways, she looked terrible. Bert should never have taken advantage of her. Now what was she going to do? The little fumble she'd had with Billy Paton, Phyllis's Indian, didn't really count as sex. Fancy him turning up again after all this time. He was a good-looking lad, but sullen. It had been over in seconds. Then he'd not even turned up for their second date. It had been so different with Bert. It had been such a lovely evening. They had gone to a cosy restaurant in Blackheath. Bert had said he loved her. He'd complimented her on her new dress. Although he'd been more keen to take it off than see it on. She was in love with Bert, that's why she had let him go so far that night, and she had sort of enjoyed it, it hadn't hurt like it had when Billy had put it in. Bert had been so gentle. Phyllis had told her that she had already done it, and that it was terribly overrated. Still, she had well and truly done it now. Pregnant and not married, what on earth was her mum going to say? When she finally had plucked up courage, Jean had been so awful. She had gone absolutely mad at her, threatening to throw her out, and she had cried all the time.

She kept asking, what on earth were people going to say?

Jean could not believe her little girl had gone and got herself pregnant. She had trusted Bert. She should have known that you couldn't trust any man where sex was concerned. She, of all people should know that after Connie's father had gone off with the blonde bingo caller that lived at Number 71 Cork Street. Jean fetched her coat, her best one, she'd purchased it from out of one of her catalogues. Admiring herself in the hall mirror, she gave a twirl round, thinking to herself, *Not bad for an old one.*

Never marrying again, she had been the only provider for the girls. She worked long hours in the local packing factory which gave her no time for herself. Neither had any opportunities arisen. Giving herself the final once over Jean opened the front door, which having dropped on its hinges had fallen to one side making it difficult to close. Jean with all her strength pulled it shut behind her, the tremor vibrating down the corridor like an earthquake. Hurrying down the steps out of the building into the pouring rain with her head down battling against the wind she walked with murderous intent towards the bus stop. By hook or by crook she was going to get Bert to make an honest woman out of Connie, before the whole of the street noticed she was in the family way.

It took her just over half an hour to reach the car showroom where Bert worked as a salesman. Her umbrella was dripping down the side of her legs and her headscarf was falling over her eyes, her mascara had run and her glasses had steamed up. She was wet and had worked herself up into a state of uncontrolled excitement. Bert was surprised when he saw Jean marching onto the car forecourt. She was waving her arms frantically at him. No way did she look like she had come to buy a car. Bert looked around. There was no way he could slip away unnoticed, or make a quick escape from this demented woman who had the look of someone who had just stepped out of an asylum. Jean marched forward unwaveringly, attacking Bert violently with her umbrella, shouting, "Connie's pregnant, Bert. She's up the duff. You've got to marry her."

Bert put his head in his hands, realising Jean would take no prisoners. He thought he should have been more careful. He did love Connie, but what on earth was he going to say to Phyllis? He'd got a bit of a thing going on with her. Phyllis had been far more accommodating about the sex and just lately he'd had many a pleasurable evening in the back of his old Morris Minor. What a mess he was in. Attempting to calm Jean down, he promised to marry Connie. Thinking to himself, wasn't life strange? Your circumstances could change in moments. He'd gone from being a Jack the lad to having a fiancée with a baby on the way. If this was becoming a responsible adult, he wasn't sure he was ready just yet. He watched Jean walk away. Now having a wedding to plan, she was hurrying along the road, her purpose to organise things as quickly as possible before Connie's pregnancy showed. Now Bert and herself had come to an agreeable solution she was going to have to pawn her mum's old gold wedding ring to help pay for it. She had a lot to do and disappeared up the road, almost running in her haste to catch the return bus. She didn't even stop to put up the remains of the broken umbrella to shield herself from the constant drizzle.

Bert wiped the rain from his forehead with his handkerchief and went back inside the dilapidated shed which he called his office, pulled a piece of headed white notepaper from the desk drawer, and took out his parker pen that had been a gift from his dad just before he'd died. He began the letter. Dear Phyllis. He just could not face her. What he was going to write, he had no idea. He certainly was not looking forward to her finding out. Having already promised Phyllis they would get married, that's why she'd been so obliging about the sex. Hell, that's where he was going. He certainly was not eager to encounter Phyllis's anger in a hurry. He could already see her growing horns.

Phyllis opened Bert's letter. She was angry, very angry. Bert hadn't the courage to tell her in person. To add insult to injury, she hadn't even been invited to the wedding. She was not going to forgive Connie for quite a while. Jimmy, her boyfriend, had just finished with her. He had no class. Even called her a money-grabbing bitch. How could she help it if she liked the nice things in life? A girl had to have standards, didn't she? She'd made up her mind, she would go to the wedding anyway. Hold her head up high. Show them all she didn't care. What a nuisance Connie getting pregnant was. She had ruined everything. For a moment, the image of her little baby girl, the secret that she kept carefully hidden from everyone, appeared just as if she were there in the room. She sat down with a thump on the kitchen chair, biting her lip in an attempt to hold back a sob which threatened to burst out. Thinking what a wonderful father Bert was going to make and how unfair life was. Folding Bert's letter carefully, she put it into her apron pocket to read when she had more time to take everything in. Suddenly changing her mind ripped it up and stamped on it. Then as if nothing had happened she resumed the job of scraping the potatoes for the evening meal just as if everything was normal.

Chapter 4

The courtship lasted three months, then Connie became pregnant with Sid. Bert with no escape route and running out of excuses proposed to Connie at Lyon's Corner House, Charing Cross. Sid became a honeymoon baby. Which everyone was supposed to believe but secretly never did.

They were married in a small church in Catford. Connie's three sisters were bridesmaids – Sally, Caroline, and Sylvia, who no one liked to point out was backward and had the mentality of a six-year-old. When the happy couple walked up the aisle, much to everyone's amusement she sang, "All I want for Christmas is my two front teeth," and proceeded to throw confetti over the vicar when Connie and Bert said their wedding vows. The girls all wore blush pink and carried yellow daisy bouquets, which everyone commented on and said how pretty they were. Connie looked a picture but a little plump. Jean found a wedding dress pattern in a women's magazine and spent a very rushed two weeks making the beautiful ivory wedding dress; it had a satin bodice which was padded slightly and slimmed at the waist and the back was buttoned all the way up with tiny pearl buttons. A long full skirt covered in machine-made lace completed the look. Jean had altered it twice already due to Connie's expanding waistline. It had a semi-bustle back and a short matching lace appliqué train. The lace was brought a from a posh shop in London with the money she received from pawning her mum's old gold ring. The buttons had come from the local market. The dress cost five pounds. Connie had a bit of a job squeezing into it but she held her breath and with Jean pulling the buttons tightly together and with the help of Aunty Maureen, they just about managed to do it up. They were exhausted with the effort. Auntie Maureen said, "If she'd left it any longer to get married, it would have been in a tent."

Bert wore his navy striped suit which he usually wore dancing. In his button hole was a yellow carnation matching the girls' bouquets. All the girls said how handsome he looked, if a tad nervous.

Phyllis wasn't sent an invitation on me Mum's request. "She was travelling," Mum said, and couldn't have made it anyway. Where, I'm not sure. But funnily enough Phyllis had turned up to the reception. How could she miss her best friend getting married? She was sure the invitation had been lost in the post.

No one had much money so the reception was held in the local church hall. Connie's sisters had spent the day before decorating the hall with pink balloons and banners, and what looked like Christmas decorations. The banners read "welcome home" which I presume, when I look back at the photographs, were from the local market, so they must have got them cheap. The cake was a strawberry Victoria sponge with a small plastic bride and groom placed carefully in the middle and covered in icing sugar. Sylvia, before the cake was even cut and the speeches had started, ate the top layer, and made herself sick over her bridesmaid's dress. Bert's sister Maureen was distraught, having made the sponge cake. Connie had hoped for something a bit more elaborate. But Jean had said, "Beggars can't be choosers and you should be grateful to Maureen for making it." It was, however, lopsided and looked like it was sinking in the middle. The groom kept falling off.

Connie said, "I hope it's not a sign of things to come!"

They played big band music all night, Glen Miller.

Everyone got up and danced, that was except the bride, who by this time was three months gone and was desperately trying to hide it with her bouquet. Although everybody knew, but tactfully didn't mention it. When she was seated her secret remained cleverly undetected, that was until Sylvia told everyone that she had a bun in the oven, not really knowing what it meant. They told her to shush and tactfully ignored her. Connie was a little cross with Bert that night, who had just one too many dances with Phyllis over the course of the evening and had to be constantly reminded by Jean just whom he was marrying.

The only time I saw Mum's face happy was in the old wedding photographs I'd found in the bureau in the front parlour. Later on, Mum cut up all her wedding photos after Dad left her for Phyllis a few years after I was born.

Chapter 5

They moved into their first house which was in Lewisham shortly after they were married. Sid was born unexpectedly in the front room on a Sunday morning. Connie by this time had given up her job in the cinema, too large to show people to their seats. She loved her job, it transported her to a world of glamour; she would pretend she was a famous film star such as Rita Hayworth, and Bert, a property tycoon or film director. Mum always did have a vivid imagination. She'd accept the bouquets, would walk up the red carpets, wear the diamonds, drive the cars and live in the mansions, only to come back to earth with an enormous kick from Sid, who, now ready to make his appearance, was causing a ruckus even before he was born. And sure enough, Sid did everything in a rush, so before the midwife had unpacked her bag and Bert had arrived home from work Sid arrived.

It had been an uncomfortable night for Connie. She hadn't been able to sleep on her back, she couldn't sleep on her front, and she couldn't sleep on her side. She was so tired. Connie knew the baby was going to come at any time. Bert had gone to work and seemed relatively unconcerned. She waddled around the kitchen feeling like a hippopotamus and thought it would be nice to see her feet again, and how unattractive she felt with Bert no longer paying her any attention. Making herself a cup of tea, she shifted herself into the rocking chair in the front parlour and sat down, picked up a magazine and started to read the first few lines. The warmth from the fire and the gentle rocking of the chair made it impossible for her to stay awake and she dropped to sleep.

An hour later terrible griping pains woke her up. Rubbing her stomach, she started to do her deep breathing, just like Jean had shown her. Panicking, Connie banged as hard as she could on the parlour wall, shouting loudly, "Leanne, the baby is coming! Hurry, I don't think I've got much time. My waters have broken."

Leanne, who was on baby alert heard the hammering through the wall, quickly pulled on her dressing gown and rushed next door, letting herself in with the key that had been given to her in case of an emergency. Connie's contractions were every two minutes, Leanne knew it wouldn't be long. Being the eldest, she had the experience of assisting with the arrival of six brothers and two sisters. Leanne helped Connie onto her hands and knees and rubbed her back. Now cursing and swearing, she was crying for her mum, saying she was never going to speak to Bert again let alone have sex with him. Leanne smiled. *That's what they all say*, she thought. Sid slipped into the world with no trouble. If only he'd taken the same path in life, causing no trouble. However, that was not meant to be. In fact, as Leanne said to me mum much later, Sid's birth, unfortunately was the start of all her troubles.

By the time the midwife had arrived Bert had returned home from work. Sid was nestled happily in his cot. Bert looked at his tiny son, gently picked him up and inspected him thoroughly, making sure everything was intact. When he looked at his thick head of black curly hair and large staring brown eyes and his dark complexion, which gave him the appearance of a foreigner, Bert wondered. He didn't take after his side of the family, and that's when he first questioned himself. Was Sid really his? He wrestled with those thoughts for the whole of his life, never wanting to believe he wasn't.

Chapter 6

Connie had an easy birth with Sid. "He popped out just like a pea," she said to her new neighbour Leanne. They spent many an hour with a cup of tea and a cream cake discussing husbands, clothes, and recipes shared from magazines when they could afford to buy them. These meals often proved to be disastrous; they would laugh hysterically when relating back to each other the result of an attempt to cook one of these posh recipes. Bert trying desperately to look as if he'd enjoyed one of these calamitous attempts. Which Connie put in front of him, waiting for his approval. Knowing for days after he would suffer with chronic indigestion.

Leanne's husband worked away, well that's what Leanne told everyone. Sid and I thought it must be on the other side of the world. He never came home at all. Not even when little Sophia died. Sid used to say it was because Leanne couldn't cook.

Sid arrived with the speed of a racing car. He was a good looking baby, healthy and strong. With large brown eyes which would stare at you angrily, and a flop of dark, thick bushy hair which made him look like a foreigner. Dad always questioned in his mind if Sid was his. He was a difficult child. Me dad never seemed to be able to handle him. He was destructive and unruly, but being me mum's first born. She would forgive him anything, loving him unconditionally. Leanne refused, in the end, to let her little daughter Sophia play with him because he could be so spiteful.

This spitefulness I was to endure all my life, always sporting a bruised shin or a black eye, always trying to hide it from Mum. She would never believe it was her beloved Sid that had started the fight. I was always the one who was in detention, while he was allowed to go out to play. This was the start of our brotherly rivalry which I had to endure all my teenage life. Until Sid joined the army. When Sid was three, Dad started up his own business. He borrowed a substantial amount of money from the bank and purchased a small plot of land. It bordered the main road into Blackheath village. "A good position for passing trade." Dad said. There was an old derelict, disused outbuilding that stood on the plot that's where they did all the repairs. Uncle Micky was roped in to help, He was good with cars but a bit of a fly boy. He could mend anything, as well as good at respraying. The old bangers looked and ran like new after he'd finished with them. We didn't have that much to do with him really. Dad told us to stay clear, because he had a bit of a temper on him, and was always in and out of trouble with the law. Mum always used to say some of it had rubbed off on Sid. Bert was the salesman out of the two. He could sell anything. He would just flash a smile, talk the good talk, and before they knew it they'd be taking home a car.

Dad's business grew from strength to strength, and he and Micky became quite prominent businessmen in Blackheath village. Uncle Jimmy joined the business later on; he wasn't really an uncle but Sid called him that cos Bert, Micky, and Jimmy were always together, either in the pub, or at the car sales buying new stock for Bert and Sons Empire. That's what Dad called it. Me mum hardly saw Dad much when he started the business. He was always late home, smelling of beer, and telling me mum he'd gone to Millwall or Shoreditch to buy a car. I don't think she believed him, especially when the smell of beer might be tinged with the faint odour of cheap perfume, when and if he climbed into bed. Mum never chastised him though. Perhaps she should have done, and things might have turned out differently.

Mum recognised the smell of the perfume, because it was the one that her friend Phyllis used to wear. Connie had never been able to afford it. Connie had lost touch with Phyllis; they didn't have a phone at that time, and for some reason since Sid had been born she'd stopped popping over. Phyllis had said to Mam, that babies weren't her thing. She much preferred travelling. However, I don't she had ever left Millwall where she lived, or even had a passport. Mum always said she was a stuck-up old cow.

Chapter 7

Sid, at the age of three was becoming too large to take out in a push chair, being much taller than boys of the same age. Connie always tried to put reins on him, but he would have none of it, and she was always losing him in a crowd especially when she shopped in Lewisham market, which was always packed with shoppers looking for a bargain. Many a time she could be seen running through the stalls frantically calling Sid's name, asking if anyone had seen a dark-haired three-year-old little boy. Sid, however, was fiercely independent, and would treat this like a game and was not at all bothered. Often finding him chatting to one of the market traders, she would sob with relief and he would just say, "Shut up, I'm a big boy now. I don't need you."

One of the stalls in the market sold young puppies and kittens, and for a few shillings you could buy one of these scruffy, slightly mangy creatures. On this Saturday morning, Sid had been found gripping a small, eight-week-old, flea-bitten black mongrel puppy. It looked like it wouldn't last the week. "Give it back," Sid had been told.

"No, it's mine," Sid had answered back.

The fat old market trader sniffed, blew his nose, tipped his battered trilby hat which had seen better days and said, "Buy the lad the pup, it's a real pedigree. Only two shillings," he said to Connie smiling as he patted Sid on the head.

Sid was hanging onto the puppy for dear life; under no circumstances was he going to let go of the wriggling little creature. Knowing she was facing a losing battle when Sid had made up his mind over something, if he didn't get his own way, all hell would break out. There was no way he was going to release the squirming puppy from his deadlock grip. Reluctantly, she handed over the two shillings from her purse which was meant to have bought Bert's steak. She took Sid by the hand, mumbling to herself, "Goodness knows what your father's going to say. He's to have egg and chips instead of a steak for dinner, and another mouth to feed in the house."

Sid was completely enthralled with the puppy,

having decided to call her Chum. He was happily gripping the squirming little mongrel closely to him in a vice-like hold, trying to stop it escaping from his arms and running off into the crowded street.

Thus brought the arrival of Chum into the house. Bert was far from pleased when he arrived home to find a flea-covered puppy, which growled aggressively at him, and a plate of egg and chips for supper. After a few disgruntled words, he disappeared that night to Millwall to buy another car, or so he said. He didn't get back till gone two in the morning.

Connie pointed out on his very late return that she hadn't known Millwall was so far away, wouldn't it have been easier to take a plane there and back? When Bert climbed into bed that night, with the lingering remains of the perfume 'Blue Grass', the very first doubt crept into her thoughts. Didn't Phyllis live in Millwall, didn't she always use 'Blue Grass'?

Chum the dog settled into the house well. She was no trouble and spent a lot of time in the back yard or just roaming the streets. By the time Chum was six months old, Sid had completely lost interest in her. The only time he took any notice of her was to cruelly pull her tail or steal a biscuit from under nose.

Chum sensibly learnt to avoid him and blend into

the household as if she wasn't there. Connie decided that Charlie need a brother or a sister. He was becoming lonely and withdrawn. Bert thought it was because he was spoilt. He didn't mix well with other children and Bert was against having another baby he said they couldn't afford it and one Sid in the family was enough for anyone to have to contend with. Connie, however though it would teach Sid how to share. So much to Bert's surprise and annoyance Connie became pregnant. Gaining several stone in weight, developing swollen ankles, her hair a mess and not wearing lipstick or painting her nails, Bert lost interest in her and took to sleeping on his own. "Being your tired and disgruntled all the time. You'll be more comfortable," he said as he moved his pyjamas into the spare room. Trying not to appear too eager.

The nine months, to Connie had seemed interminably long. Sid was more difficult and demanding than usual and she was now feeling very uncomfortable as the baby was overdue by two weeks; the midwife had given instructions to Connie to eat something spicy and take a long brisk walk. In the hope it would start the contractions.

The weather had got progressively worse. The morning had turned into an extremely cold one. Frost covered the ground and the tops of the cars looked like they were covered in icing sugar, the damp causing a chill to creep deep into your bones. Connie wrapped herself up well to protect herself from the wind that had sprung up, making it difficult to walk. Deciding to catch the bus and take Sid to visit Bert at his showroom. Which he loved to do. Connie thought perhaps she'd make more of an effort. She combed her hair and tried to remove the tangles. Sprayed herself with the eau de toilette Lily Of The Valley which Bert had bought for her at Christmas. Searched in the bottom of her handbag and found the lipstick 'Glamour Red'. Now old, the tip broken and its luscious shine long gone. Wiping it clean with her hanky she applied it to her lips and pursed them together in a kiss. Disappointed, she gave a large tearful gulp, it hadn't achieved quite the desired effect that she'd hoped for. It was the one she'd always worn up the Pally which made you look as if you were pouting. Bert loved it , said it made her look sexy. She wasn't looking very sexy now she thought.

Connie took Sidney's hand and they walked up the street to the bus stop. The temperature had dropped considerably bringing an acute chill in the air. The snow now turning to ice was making it slippery underfoot , much to Sid's delight who purposefully skidded dangerously along the pavement nearly pulling

Connie over. She wrapped her coat tightly around her in an attempt to protect herself from the bitter wind that had sprung from nowhere and told Sid to be quiet as she tried to button his coat while he wriggled and squirmed in protest. He was being his usual difficult self and his constant chattering and questioning why was this? And why was that? was beginning to get on her nerves. The bus was twenty minutes late and he'd become fidgety and very rude to the other people in the queue, so she was very grateful when it finally arrived. The showroom was a good ten minutes' brisk walk from the bus stop and Connie hurried along, striding out with look of grim determination on her face in the hope that there might be some sign of activity from the baby. *Funny!* she thought when she got there. The 'closed' sign was up. Bert had not said he was going out. Connie finding the door unlocked pushed it open and gasped in disbelief. Bert with trousers down had Phyllis sprawled across the desk with knickers round her ankles, and they were at it like rabbits. Connie shoved Sid behind her back , holding her hands tightly across his eyes in the hope he wouldn't see what was going on, yelling at Bert across the room. "How could you both?" she said, and at that precise moment her waters broke. Connie looked at the puddle that had appeared surprisingly beneath her feet. Realising the arrival of the new baby was imminent, Bert pulled up his trousers as quickly as was humanly possible, trying repeatedly, but unsuccessfully to fasten his belt in his haste to get dressed. Phyllis pulled up her knickers at the same time as making a backward retreat out of the door, desperately apologising as she went. "I'm so sorry, Connie; forgive me, it's all Bert's fault. I only came to buy a car."

Connie by this time had become hysterical. Sid was sobbing loudly and Bert had his head in his hands. "Forgive me, Connie," he said. "It was just the once. I don't know what came over me, luv. Calm down, we've got to get you to the hospital." Bert hastily brought the car round to the front of the showroom, apologising profoundly the whole time as he bundled little Sid, kicking and struggling, into the back seat. Then helping Connie into the front passenger, he put his foot down on the accelerator and drove as fast as he could to Blackheath hospital. Connie's contractions were coming every few minutes, and by the time they had arrived at the hospital, Connie was in the early stages of labour.

Three hours later, cursing and swearing and with no sign of Bert on the horizon, the baby arrived. Connie took one look at her new son. Tiny, blue eyes, no hair and weighing just six pounds, said to the nurse, "He's not a looker, this one, not like our Sid. We'll call him Robert after me dad." From that day I was known as little Bob. Bert came to collect us later the next day. He had a large bunch of flowers, a gigantic white teddy bear, and a very sheepish grin on his face. "You did well, Connie, least this one looks like me."

Connie banned Phyllis from being mentioned in the house again. That was until a few years later when all hell was to break loose.

Chapter 8

Sid hated my arrival right from the start. He was always jealous of any affection me dad or mum might give me. He was repeatedly told off for rocking the cradle too hard or for pulling the covers up too high. Right from the start I had one ally, and that was Chum. She guarded and protected me against anything that put me in harm's way, growling at Sid and sometimes even dad when they ventured to pick me up. We became inseparable. Mum would say, "You wouldn't see one without the other." She was the only one allowed to get near me without her snarling. As I grew up she slept beside my bed or with her head on my legs, when I slept on the floor. This used to annoy Sid terribly, but he was always too frightened of Chum and left her well alone. She was a lioness protecting a cub, always on duty, although luckily she never produced any of her own. Dad used to laugh and call Sid a coward, but it was noted he carefully avoided Chum if she was anywhere near me.

When I turned three, me mum went back to work two days a week. Sid was at school, or meant to be. He secretly always managed to skip lessons. This was never discovered till much later on, much to Dad's anger that he couldn't read or write because he had never attended. Leanne next door used to look after us, she would make mine and Sid's tea when we got home from school and mum collected us after she finished her shift. Sadly, Leanne's daughter Sophia had died when she was two. She'd caught a bad case of chicken pox. Leanne had been very brave. We were too small at the time to go to the funeral and Mum told us that Sophia had joined the angels. Sid and I thought this was the church choir and couldn't understand why she never came home. Me mum used to say she'd send Sid to join the same choir if he didn't behave himself. I didn't think he'd be allowed. He never could hold a tune. Sadly, Leanne couldn't have any more children. Mum said she could share Sid and me. I'm not sure that was really what Leanne had in mind. She would have rather had one of her own, but that was never to happen, unfortunately for her.

Mum was thrilled she finally had a job in the local department store selling Elizabeth Arden. She looked so glamorous. I always remember the overpowering smell of the scent "Valencia". Mum would kiss us goodbye and tell us to be good boy's. The fragrant smell of oranges would linger in the room way after she'd left. Whenever I used to smell "Valencia" it always reminded me of mum.

We hated going to Leanne's. She cried all the time, and always tried to cuddle us. Sid would always push her away. I used to grin and bear it but found it very unpleasant because she always smelt of curry. Dad seemed to have settled back into family life and given up seeing Phyllis on the side. That's what me mum thought. How wrong she was.

*

On Mum's return to work. Friday was mum's payday and she would bring us home fish and chips. Sid liked a gherkin, so Mum would bring one back specially for him. If I asked, I was never allowed any extras. Sid was Mum's favourite. When we settled down in front of the telly to watch a film, it was usually a romantic one. We were never allowed to watch the horror films, Mum said it would give us nightmares. We were one of the only ones in the street to have a telly. Mum used to like to watch Vanity Fair. It was a fashion programme. Sid and me preferred to watch Tele-crime where the viewer had to solve the misdemeanour, it was a real whodunit. Mum would always switch it off and say, "We wouldn't sleep if we watched that rubbish." When dad left he took the telly and we didn't get another one for ages afterwards.

It was a Monday that mum discovered dad and Phyllis together again. Sid was turning into a bit of a ruffian. I had just started school. Sid was meant to take me there and make sure I was safely inside the playground gate, he never did though, he would just hand me over to anyone that he thought might be heading in that direction. Chum would walk with us; she was looking grey round the mouth now, but she was still dedicated in her protection duty. Always there waiting for me at four o'clock when I came out of school. I felt safe with her to accompany me. Sid could never be found, he would be off on one of his secret missions, but he would tell me mum that he had met me from school and brought me home. Sometimes a few of the boys would follow me. They would yell at me, "Baby Bob's got his babysitter," but always kept a respectful distance from Chum. They discovered when they came too close she would wrinkle her nose and a low grumbling sound would come from her stomach. They learnt that getting too near to her when they tried to pinch my sweets would end with a nipped finger or a torn blazer. Many times, Mum had an irate mother knocking on the door waving a ripped item of clothing, demanding money and blaming Chum, but Mum would look through the curtains and wouldn't open it. If they tackled her in the street, she would deny any knowledge that Chum was ours.

Connie felt unwell. Looking closely in the mirror she pinched her cheeks, but realising she still looked pale dabbed some lipstick on them. Her legs felt like jelly and she had the feeling they might give way. Releasing an enormous sigh. *I do hope I'm not coming down with flu*, she thought. Resigning herself, because of the money she owed there was no way she could take the day off, especially as Bert was in complete ignorance to the debt she had to her surprise accumulated - he never asked where the extra luxuries came from. The perfume she wore was from the market. The "Valencia" she loved was too expensive for her to buy. When she had the chance. Connie would spray herself with the tester bottle at work, sometimes she would slip a small free sample into her pocket in the hope it would go unnoticed. Bert, she had found out over the years, was not a generous man. If he thought it was necessary he would let her purchase the item she wanted, but a new dress, or household accessories were considered to be frivolous and thought an unnecessary addition to the household expenditure and should not be included in the housekeeping budget. Bert always told her off for spending too much money. Connie always had to hide her new purchases from him. Or said to him that Jean had given them to her. Over the years, she became well known in the local pawn shop. Though eventually she didn't have that much left to pawn and struggled trying to buy any of the items back. Bert never knew that anything was missing. Not even his gold watch. He was happy just as long as he wasn't bothered for any money.

Connie made her way to the bus stop, by this time she was late. The queue was long and the Number 14 bus that took her directly to work was running twenty minutes behind schedule. When the bus arrived, it was already full. Connie was just about to push her way onto the platform when the conductor rushed forward, holding his hand up in front of him. "We're full, luv," he'd said, "Not even standing room. You will have to catch the next one." With that, he dinged the bell, and shouted, "Tickets please!" And Connie watched the bus as it moved pulled slowly away and disappeared around the corner. What now? She would be much too late to clock on. Feeling no better, *I'll go sick*, she thought. *I might even still get paid.*

Deciding to avoid Lewisham in case she bumped into anyone from work, she took a slow stroll into Blackheath village looking for a little coffee shop where she could have a hot chocolate and a bun. It might take away the queasiness she was feeling. Blackheath was up and coming at the time, and coffee shops were starting to appear in the village. It was considered a real treat to have afternoon tea in one because everything was so expensive on their menus. However, it was very vogue to be seen having coffee or tea in one of these drinking establishments and she just loved to be fashionable. Wandering up the little quaint high street, glancing in the windows, admiring everything she couldn't afford, wistfully thinking what she bye if she had some spare money, she branched off the main street and wandered down a small side road knowing there was a coffee shop called the Cup and Saucer which had just opened. Today they were promoting a free slice of cake if you bought a pot of tea. Checking in her purse just to make sure she had enough money, she pushed open the door and looked around for a window seat, so she could waste half an hour watching all the coming and goings of the people hurrying up down the street.

The coffee shop was full. The weather outside, now

considerably colder had brought a crowd of people in to sample the steaming hot creamy coffee and the luxurious free carrot cake that sat inviting you to eat it in the window. The cafe was bustling. Every seat appeared to be taken; she happened to notice two people seated tucked in a darkened corner of the cafe. They were holding hands across the table, so completely absorbed, their attention focused only on one another, they failed to notice or look up when the doorbell tinkled and Connie entered. She stood motionless, fixed to the spot, powerless to move her feet it was as if she had stepped into a pool of quicksand that was sucking her in and pulling her down. She felt any moment she would disappear beneath the floorboards never to be seen again, almost wishing she could. She held her breath, unable to believe who she saw directly in front of her. The woman, who dressed immaculately, was wearing a fox-fur tie around her neck, a navy spotted suit, high heels and stockings with seams that went right up the back of the leg. Her hair was a dark brunette, concealed under a little navy beret. She could have stepped out of any London fashion magazine, but Connie recognised her immediately. Their hands were clasped together across the table, laughing and joking at some shared secret intimacy. For a brief second the man looked away from his companion towards the door and he met Connie's gaze. He stopped talking immediately. The look of utter desolation and abandonment that met his stare was to haunt Bert for the rest of his life, realising with a wave of sheer panic that rendered him completely silent, he was looking at his wife. He had been found out.

Before Bert could rise from the table, Connie, released from her trance as if by an invisible hand waving a magic wand which had given her the ability to move her arms and legs, ran from the coffee shop, upsetting a table and chair and knocking coffee and cake flying. Bert was not fast enough to stop her from leaving. He followed her out the door and watched sadly, realising the consequences of his liaison as she ran out of sight. Turning to go back into the shop he looked down at his feet then bent down and picked up her purse and the few coins which now lay scattered across the floor which she had dropped in her hurry to leave.

That really was the end of life as we knew it. When Dad finally arrived home, his bags had been packed and were sitting waiting at the front door. We didn't see Dad again for quite some time. He moved in with Phyllis who had a flat in Millwall. Dad's little parting gift to us all was me sister, Sally, who was a very unexpected surprise. Especially to Mum. Dad had been the love of her life; overnight Mum changed from being jolly, laughing, and compassionate to being miserable, depressed, and irritated with all around her. She stopped dying her hair, putting on lipstick, and with the impending birth of another baby and no dad around, became very bad tempered with Sid and me. Money was scarce in the household, making it difficult to make the bills match Mum's disposable income.

Our lunch boxes me mum had once put sweets and pieces of Cadbury's chocolate in, now contained half a sandwich. We were left unsupervised for long periods of time. Always a small boy, now thin and undernourished, my trousers hung on my short legs. Sid took to thieving off the stalls in Lewisham market and always managed to bring home a bit of good meat for Sunday dinner. I saved mine for Chum, otherwise I think she might have perished. Although Leanne next door always found a bone to give to her or a few leftover scraps so that she didn't go unfed for long. Mum lost interest in us. So, left to our own devices, we stirred up quite a bit of trouble in the neighbourhood and became very unpopular, Sid more than me. People were frightened of Sid, so he didn't get told off that much. I was always being marched home by the ear by an irate neighbour for me mum to issue some form of discipline. Mum was taken into hospital early when Sally was born. Being a breach birth, it was touch and go if the midwife could turn her. Blue and not breathing was her entrance into the world. I often wondered if me mum would take to her after all the trouble she'd caused. But when the nurse placed the tiny little squiggly baby that Sid said looked like an alien in her arms, me Aunty Sally said you could see her melt.

Sally was born with a head of bright red hair. Mum said it was from Dad's side of the family, they had originated from Ireland and she should have come out dancing, which made us all laugh. Sally had the nature of an angel; everyone loved her and she loved everyone. Even Sid had a bit of a soft spot, but he would never let on. Dad came round to see the baby when she was born and left fifty pounds on the table. He asked if he could come back. Mum said no, she wasn't ready to forgive him just yet. Mum would have liked to throw it back at him, but we needed the money so she took it, and we all ate out on fish and chips after he left and had a bit of a party.

Mum found it very difficult with a new baby. Leanne next door helped out and babysat when me mum went back to work. A few months after Sally had been born Phyllis met Mum in Lewisham high street, pushing the old blue cross pram that had been Sophia's next door. Leanne had always kept it just in case but sadly she never needed it again, so gave it to Mum. Phyllis tried to be pleasant but me mum turned round and went back up the street. Phyllis had looked in the pram. For a moment she remembered her own little baby girl and walked back to the flat sobbing. She never told Dad why. He always put it down to women's problems. Phyllis always wanted her own children; none came along so she was always very jealous of Mum and us. Mum used to say, "Dad must have tied a knot in it." What this meant, Sid and I weren't very sure, until one of the older boys taught us the facts of life. Sid was keen to practice, but I thought it was disgusting, that was until I reached puberty and by that time I couldn't wait to catch up with Sid.

Mum learnt to accept the situation over the years, although she never fully forgave Phyllis. She learnt that as she couldn't change what had happened she had to put up with it and make the best of it. Mum was still quite a looker, and it wasn't long after that Uncle Jimmy started showing an interest in her. He became a permanent addition to the family without anyone taking much notice. He just sort of moved in. After a while we couldn't remember a time when he hadn't been there.

Chapter 9

Young Bob was becoming more like Bert every day. Sid was just Sid. Phyllis often looked back on her life wondering if she had done the right thing. Losing her best friend over a man was not the brightest thing she had ever done. Not being able to have Bert's children had been a terrible disappointment to her. Being discovered in the coffee shop that day, what an upset that had caused. Connie turning the table and chairs over and running off like that. Bert turning up on her doorstep that night with just a suitcase and asking if he could move in. Phyllis hadn't really planned on things being so permanent. Funny how things worked out. Connie never really spoke to her after that. She had tried once when Sally had been born; meeting her in the street that day had been quite a shock, and then to be completely ignored. Connie had never known her secret, neither had Bert. Phyllis had concealed it from everyone. Uncle Jimmy found out years later when Dad died. Phyllis felt she should tell someone, just in case the child ever came looking for her, but she never did. Not while she was still alive. It was only years later we discovered the truth.

Phyllis was forward for a girl. Connie was a little more reserved in her attempts to meet and date boys. Now sixteen, they had become very attractive young women. Much to Jean's annoyance they paid no heed to her concerns for the welfare of the two of them. They were always late home and paid no attention to her constant reminders to be on their guard against young men. In Jean's eyes, they were only after one thing. Every Friday night they would get ready together. Phyllis with a wet tea cloth over her head would bend precariously backwards over the ironing board. Connie would then endeavour to straighten her curly brunette hair by ironing it flat. Usually unsuccessfully as being so thick it was virtually impossible to do so. Sometimes they would talk so much Connie would forget to remove the iron and the smell of frizzled burning hair would circulate round the flat and creep into the corridor outside. The neighbours always thought the flat was on fire, the girls couldn't stop themselves shrieking with laughter. Mr Parker who lived next door, who was extremely miserable with no sense of humour, would often bang on the door, shouting, "Fire!" And everyone would evacuate the building. When the unintentional fire drill was over and they returned to the flat Connie would try and convince Phyllis that the two inches that she had cut from the bottom of her hair which had left it uneven and lopsided, was the latest fashion. Phyllis however, didn't quite believe her and in an attempt to hide the damage would then sit with very large rollers in her hair while they sat discussing the local talent , trying to put the curl back in her hair which they had spent the last hour trying to remove.

Connie was fed up. She always seemed to have her eye on the same boy as Phyllis. Billy Paton was one of them. What a looker. Tall, wavy hair, and dark skinned, he'd never known his father and people used to say that his dad had been an Indian who'd worked on the docks who had just skipped the country one day and left his mum up the duff. Billy always denied this, though Phyllis said the true story was that his dad had been caught thieving in the docks, got into a fight and been thrown into the water and drowned. He was a remarkably good-looking boy. Thick dark brown hair which he wore quite long. This made him stand apart from the other boys. He had large, brown, piercing eyes that seemed to stare right through you. He had a cocky stance about him, and he flirted shamelessly with all the girls but never dated. There was an air of mystery about him that girls found very attractive. Billy never let on what his true heritage was and Connie said she thought he'd come from royalty, He looked full of eastern promise and they would giggle to each other. Phyllis adored him. She wrote his name everywhere on any scrap of paper she could find. She ate, slept, and dreamt about him. In fact, Connie was finding it pretty boring. Although Billy once or twice had given her a cheeky look and was quite good looking. She wouldn't mention it to Phyllis that he had asked her for a date. Best not make her jealous.

They had been to a birthday celebration that Friday. It was late when they thought about returning home. Connie knew if they didn't leave the party soon Jean would be on the warpath. There apparently had been some nasty incidents. None of which anyone seemed to want to talk about. Although there had been lots of rumours flying around about a sex attacker, so they were very appreciative when Billy offered to see them home. What a gentleman he was. They left Connie at the end of her road. Phyllis lived in the next block of flats, Germaine House. Cheerfully waving Connie goodbye, Phyllis watched her walk away, delighted that she now had Billy all to herself. Trembling with nerves,

Phyllis let him take her hand which he held very tightly in his. Looking up at him, she could see he was agitated Phyllis felt uneasy he yanked her along walking quickly and she found it difficult to keep up with him. Her shoes which she had insisted on borrowing from Connie were too big for her and one slipped from her foot. Billy's grip was becoming uncomfortable, his hand squeezing hers so hard her arm had gone numb. He increased the pace.

Phyllis had never had a real boyfriend before and was starting to feel scared. Billy had not said a word, and Phyllis repeatedly asked him, "Where are we going?" He was leading her away from the front of the building where she lived. Trying to pull herself free her, requests had now turned into desperate pleas to let go of her hand. Billy was a strong lad and her helpless attempts were futile. His nails were digging into her skin drawing blood. She fell forwards unable to keep up with him. He dragged her along the floor, her knees burning in pain as they scraped across the ground. She thought she would burst into flames. Phyllis began to cry. Billy tightened his hold. "Please, Billy, what are you doing? Let me go. I want to go home."

Phyllis was sobbing uncontrollably.

"You're a slut," he said. "And sluts get what they

deserve."

Phyllis attempted to scream, but nothing came from her mouth – it was as if it had been stapled together and her body wrapped with bandages and mummified which prevented her from struggling. Billy pulled her to the back of the flats and shoved her violently onto the stony gravel, staring down at her. There were no security lights, they had been smashed and never replaced. But a glow of light creeping through the blind of a ground floor flat shone directly across Billy's face, allowing Phyllis to see clearly his look of disgust and contempt as he pulled up her skirt, wrenched down her knickers and raped her.

It was over in minutes, degrading but not brutal. She had been unable to struggle, just lying still as if she had been embalmed. "I'll kill you," he said, "if you tell anyone." Then twisting her arm back just to make sure Phyllis knew that he was deadly serious, he put his hand over her mouth. Taking a small flick knife from his pocket, he held it up to her throat, slowly running the blade from left to right. Then he stood up, pulled up his trousers and fastened his belt, looked nonchalantly around then walked away as if he were out for an afternoon stroll. He cared not one iota with what had just taken place, never even bothering to look back.

Phyllis was unhurt but deep in shock her whole body numb, paralysed by fear. The silence of the night smothering her like a blanket. No one to hear her cries, or see her distress. She sat for a while in complete denial of what had just taken place. After what to her seemed like hours she struggled slowly to her feet. Looking around for her handbag but unable to find it with the weariness of an old lady she made her way home. All she could think of was that her new skirt was now ruined and she would never be able to wear it again. Not that she would want to.

"I've been robbed. He came from behind and stole me bag," she said, falling into her mum's arms. She had an inexplicable dread of telling Lillian, her mum, the truth. Phyllis never saw Billy again. People said that he'd gone looking for his dad in some foreign country, but Phyllis knew better and hoped she would never see him again. She was too ashamed to tell anyone what had happened. Not even Connie. If she had done Connie would never have gone out with Billy a couple of years later, when he had turned up unexpectedly out of the blue on a visit to see his old mum. Connie's whole life might have taken a different course of events. And Sid might never have been born.

Connie said, "What a shame Billy has gone," and what a nice fella he was, for walking them both home that night.

Over the next few months. Connie kept commenting on how fat Phyllis seemed to be getting, and if she didn't stop eating she was never going to get a lad to take her out. Phyllis just couldn't fit into any of her dresses. She felt tired and sick all the time. Perhaps she just needed a tonic to buck her up. This morning she looking really under the weather, her mum said to her as she went to work, "Best stay in bed."

The event which pulled at her heart and was kept secretly locked in Phyllis's memory for the whole of her life started with her feeling queasy and unsteady on her feet. As she tottered into the kitchen the first pain gripped her. Looking down, she realised there was a large pool of liquid, which, without explanation had appeared on the floor beneath her. Her breathing became laboured and she began to tremble violently. Her stomach began doing cartwheels, it was like the most aggressive indigestion she had ever experienced. The second pain and then the third came, each more violent than the other. She hung on to the side of the table with both hands to stop herself falling to the floor.

Having an almighty urge to push down, she squeezed hard, the pain sending her almost unconscious. Never had she experienced anything like it in her life. It was worse even than the pain she'd felt when her Dad had died and the school had called her into the office and told her that he had suffered a fatal heart attack. The pain she had felt then was unbearable. The pain she felt now was equally excruciating, and she bit hard into her hand to stop herself from screaming out loud. Phyllis had absolutely no idea that she was pregnant. Placing her hands between her legs, she pulled tentatively. She felt this strange thing emerging from between them. Giving another almighty push, she looked down thinking she would see all of her insides lying on the kitchen floor.

The very tiny dark-skinned baby girl quickly entered into the world like a child that had slithered out of control down a water slide, covered in a wax-like substance. The baby was small and very early, giving her the appearance of a child's china doll rather than a newborn infant. Phyllis sat very still for a little while; she must be having a terrible nightmare and she would wake up any moment. Perhaps it was all just a dream. Finally, she managed to stop shaking. Putting her hand on the baby's head, she felt the warmth beneath her fingertips of this new life that had forced its way into the world with every intention of surviving. She knew then that this was real. How would she tell her mum? Knowing her mum, she would be disowned and thrown out. She would never forgive her. The wrinkled, squirming, tiny infant had started making a small bleating noise. Phyllis wiped the baby clean, unable to believe what had just happened. The baby, although premature seemed to be breathing normally, and when Phyllis placed her finger into the infant's mouth, the little girl sucked automatically, expecting milk. Phyllis made up her mind. Taking the kitchen scissors from out of the drawer, she cut the umbilical cord and separated herself from the crying infant. Panicking and now sobbing between breaths, she got to her feet, pulling an old overcoat on that hung in the hallway which her mum used to put the rubbish out in every morning. Not bothering to get out of her bloodied nightgown, she put on her shoes, went to the bathroom and flushed the after birth down the toilet. Then carefully put the baby in an empty pink pillowcase she found in the wash basket.

Leaving the flat, she walked as quickly as she could in the direction of the convent, the baby concealed beneath her coat, away from any prying eyes. The

Catholic convent was a good fifteen minutes away and she walked looking straight ahead in complete control and with a purpose. She could feel the warmth of the breathing body against herself, the baby girl every so often whimpering like a newborn puppy and snuggling nearer to her, trying to find milk. Phyllis was always a little frightened of the nuns. So it was with great nervousness she approached the convent and went up to the front door. She placed the baby at the top of the concrete steps and rang the bell twice. Then descended the steps two at a time and ran across the road. Trying hard to conceal herself, she stood watching from the shadows. The convent door opened. A young nun appeared, glanced down, picked up the wriggling bundle and held it closely to her, then looked from left to right. Seeing no one, she turned round and went back inside. Phyllis sobbed all the way home. Her mum returned from work and said, how much better Phyllis looked and a day in bed had done her the world of good.

A few days later Connie and Phyllis read in the local paper about a dark-skinned baby girl, possibly Indian, that had been left on the convent steps. The papers said if anyone knew anything at all to come forward. No one ever did. Connie said, "How terribly sad." The little girl was never mentioned again. Phyllis tried never to think about her and pushed any thought of her out of her mind. Just as if it had never happened. Her mum always did ask the question, where had the pillowcase gone? She said, "Isn't it funny that the laundry basket has eaten it the same as Henry's black socks?" Henry being Phyllis's elder brother, who brought his washing home now and again for her mum to do. Years later Phyllis had tried to find out where the baby had gone. The nuns refused to tell her. Phyllis always hoped her little girl had been given a happy childhood, and that maybe she'd been adopted by some rich family.

When Phyllis was dying she had said to Jimmy it had been the biggest regret of her life, not telling the truth that night. She had always wished she had kept the baby girl. Always hoping she would find her before she died. Never having any children of her own with Bert, it had left a sadness in her that had never been resolved. We were never very kind to Phyllis. When I realised why she had always been so jealous of me mum and us kids I felt very sad for her. I wondered if many families had such secrets locked in their past never to be revealed. I wished we had been nicer to Phyllis, but it was all too late by then.

Chapter 10

Nikki, meaning 'little' and 'small'. The nuns had named her that. They found her on the top steps of the convent, barely alive and weighing only five pounds. There had been no note, no blanket. All she had was the pink pillowcase that she had been found in. It was old and the lace frill around the edge had started to fray. Nikki ran her fingers over the cotton material, stroking it lightly. She tried to imagine what had driven her mother to abandon her. She had grown into an attractive young woman, petite in build and at twenty-eight could still have passed for a teenager. Her long, shiny, thick hair rested on her shoulders like a horse's mane. Her tiny hands and feet reminded you of a China doll, her glowing brown skin and dark hazelnut eyes made her appear foreign. There was a melancholy aura surrounding her, a certain sadness that she was never able to leave behind. Brushing her hair gently, she looked in the mirror and stood wondering once again, if she bore any resemblance to her birth mother or father.

Today was her birthday. Or what her step-mum called her Anniversary Day. The day that she had been found on the convent steps. Her step-mum had decided her real birthday would be on the day that they had adopted her, as it had been a great day for a celebration, telling Nikki it had been the happiest day of her life. Today, however, was always remembered with great sadness. Always questioning what terrible course of events had driven a mother to abandon her newborn baby on the steps of a convent. How she wished she could meet her and ask her why. Today was the day she lit a candle in the church beside the convent. She would leave a little message at the base, hoping one day it might be found. She had been doing this for fifteen years, having made a promise to herself that she would continue as long as she could. The note read: 'Mum, I forgive you. All I want to know is why?' Attached to the note was a tiny piece of lace belonging to the pink pillowcase that she had been found in.

Mary, her adoptive mother, called upstairs, "Breakfast is ready, darling. You'll be late for work."

Nikki ran down the stairs, and grabbed a piece of toast from off the table. "Sorry Mum," she said, kissing her on the cheek and smiling as she ran out the door, "I'll be really late."

Mary looked out the window and her eyes followed her beautiful daughter as she ran up the road. When Brian, her stepfather, died she had been a wonderful help to her. Had even moved back into the house to be there for her when she had what Nikki called her dark moments. When she was absolutely sure that she was out of sight, she sat down on the kitchen chair and took from her pocket the official-looking brown envelope that had arrived addressed to her in the post earlier in the week. She laid it flat on the table and pressed out the creases and put on her reading glasses. The letter was from the South London Adoption Agency. After all these years Nikki's real mother had come forward. She wanted to arrange a meeting. A heart-wrenching letter of explanation was enclosed.

My name is Phyllis Hill. I am your birth mother. A day has not gone by when I have not thought of you, I have never forgotten you and have always held you close to my heart. I never married or had other children. I have a lifelong partner,

Bert, with whom I have been very happy. I would like to know that you have been happy. The day I left you on the steps of the convent was the hardest thing I have ever done, but I was unmarried and your father half Indian, who now I believe is on the other side of the world. I could not keep you. My mother would have disowned me. I had no way of supporting you. If you could please feel it in your heart to forgive me, I would love to see your face before I die and hold you close. This time I will never let you go. I am sure you have grown from a beautiful baby into a wonderful young woman. I would like to hold you in my arms and hear about your childhood, your dreams and your achievements. I would like to know you. Let me be a part of your life. Although I would not wish to upset your parents. I am still your mother and you will always be my daughter till the day I die.

All my love, your birth mother Phyllis.

Mary read and reread the letter, removed her glasses then ripped the letter into a thousand little pieces, and pushed them forcibly into the dustbin, making sure they were carefully hidden by covering them over with the remains of breakfast. The bin men were due this morning. *You had your chance, Phyllis Hill. Nikki's my daughter now.* And with that thought held firmly in her mind she filled the kettle and made another cup of tea.

Nikki never knew her birth mother had tried to get in touch and forever wondered what her real mother had been like. She was none the wiser when Phyllis sadly died.

Chapter 11

Over the next few years, life became difficult for us. Dad stopped paying the mortgage. He said he couldn't afford to run two houses. So mum, Sid, me and Sally moved into rented. It was a small terraced house in Blackheath. Two attic bedrooms, one of which I shared with Sid and the other mum and Sally slept in. There was a front and back parlour, one of which mum eventually made into a bedroom for her and Jimmy. The kitchen led out to a small backyard where we used to hang the washing. We had an outside toilet which seemed a long way away from the house if you were caught short. I took to doing a paper round to earn a bit of extra money. Chum, although old, would accompany me in the mornings.

Sid was more inventive with his attempt at earning money. Sid and I used to read all the magazines before I delivered them so they were quite scruffy by the time I put them through anyone's letterbox. George up the road used to have a garden magazine delivered once a month. He loved the garden, and I would always be told to keep off his grass when delivering the papers. His garden was large and it took up all his time. He was so proud of it and he'd once won a prize for having the best garden in Blackheath. He always gave me descriptions of every plant, herb, and weed each time I delivered his paper. Sid had a marvellous idea. One Saturday morning he climbed over George's fence It was very cold and still dark. The first frost of winter had arrived leaving the ground hard and the grass crisp. Sid had with him a sack and spade. He spent the next hour digging up plants and bushes and putting them carefully into the sack. George was sound asleep completely unaware that his garden had been invaded and his shrubs were being stolen. By the time I delivered George his morning paper, Sid was safely home and the plants carefully concealed under the bed in our attic room. The only evidence that Sid had left the house were his very muddy boots. He had a difficult job explaining to mum where all the dirt on the parlour floor had come from. I thought the plants would die as it was colder in our attic than in George's garden. But they survived the week carefully hidden from mum. Who would have been furious if she had found them.

The following Saturday Sid banged on George's door. In Mum's shopping basket he had the plants he'd stolen. He told George Mum was selling them to make some extra money because Sally desperately needed an operation. George was happy to contribute. He bought back his own plants for half a crown. He never caught on they were from his very own garden.

A few months later George met Mum in the street and asked how Sally's operation had gone. When Mum found out the truth she put Sid and me under house arrest for a few weeks. We never took the chance of doing it again. Sid never shared the half a crown with me, so I threatened to tell our mum if he ever did it again. Although she was cross I heard her giggling about it to Uncle Jimmy for quite some time afterwards, it tickled her sense of humour. She never let on to us she found it funny though.

Chapter 12

Mum returned to work as an usherette at the local cinema. We needed the money. We would creep in the fire exit on a Saturday afternoon. Sometimes we were lucky and had a bag of popcorn to share. Sid, however, always ate most of it and I got the bits at the end. I gave up fighting him for it. I used to love the westerns with John Wayne and would always shoot my way out of the cinema riding a big white stallion. Sid was always the gangster and would smoke a big pretend cigar and talk in an American accent. He'd march me out the cinema with a gun in my back.

For the rest of the day we would just hang around doing nothing in particular with Harry and Mickey who lived up the road from us. We had this little clubhouse in Harry's shed at the bottom of his garden. We called it the camp. On our way home from the cinema we'd pick up any dog ends we'd find. Back at camp we'd fill an acorn with the tobacco that we'd removed from the dog end. Then light it up and smoke it through a straw, coughing away like little old men. That was until Harry's mum caught us. She thought the shed was on fire. So we had to look for another camp. If the weather was good, we used to play knock down ginger. We'd tie a piece of black cotton which was just strong enough to lift the knocker on the front door, but not thick enough to be seen. All four of us would then sit in the bushes and hide. Our hands over our mouths, trying to be really quiet and trying not to laugh too loudly, we'd pull the knocker up and down with the cotton. When someone came to the door to answer it, there would be no one there. We would do this several times, and would sit giggling until they eventually realised they'd been duped and traced the cotton back to where we were hiding. We would then run like hell, being chased down the street. We would laugh so much that we couldn't breathe, until we reached a place of safety. We would do this time and time again until we were caught and were marched back to Mum, who put us on toilet duty for some time.

There was a large field at the back of our house where we played. This is where we made our new camp. It was a building site really, everybody used to dump their rubbish there – old tables and chairs, old beds, in fact anything they didn't have any use for. They also stored the prefabs there for building the temporary housing. Mum had forbidden us to play there but that just made it more exciting. In the school holidays, we would all meet at the camp and plan the rest of the day. Sid and Harry had been standing on a large piece of wooden prefab, I was in the middle and Harry and Sid were jumping up and down on each end. Each time they landed with a crash on the end of the plank I jetted high into the air like a rocket. It was like a seesaw, up and down we went singing rude songs at the top our voices, enjoying the moment which was short lived.

All of a sudden there was a loud crack; there was nothing beneath my feet. The wood had broken in two pieces and I fell down the middle. Trying to save myself, I grabbed the side of a wooden panel, catching my hand on a large nail. My little finger was hanging. Nearly detached from my hand.

Blood spurted everywhere. Sid and Harry thought I'd cut an artery.

They ran off; they knew they'd be in big trouble from me mum. Holding my little finger in Dad's white handkerchief, which was at least clean, and trying hard not to look at it, I went to find Mum. I found her polishing the front door. She removed the hanky and my finger dripped with blood all over the step. I thought she would pass out, luckily the first-aid course that she'd taken at work proved very helpful. Next door Uncle Bill, we called him that although he wasn't a proper uncle, had a freezer box. He was quite rich and Sid and I had always hoped Mum and him would get together. It certainly was not for him trying or us pushing them together. He made several unsuccessful attempts at asking me mum out. Then gave up. She would have none of it, saying he was far too old. We said to Mum that it didn't matter. Sid said he'd die soon and then we'd all be rich. Mum told Sid not to be so wicked.

Uncle Bill wrapped my hand in the ice which he kept for his six o'clock gin and tonic. Then he drove Mum and me to Lewisham Hospital. They reattached my little finger in a two-hour operation and I had to remain in hospital for two days. Although it was successful, my little finger never straightened and always curled. Sid always took the rise out of me and said as well as acting like the queen, I now looked like her.

Me mum said it looked like I had real manners and was a young man of sophistication. Harry and Sid were put on detention for two weeks, but somehow still managed to slip out. Mum was still lacking in her disciplinary technique and Sid and me were always in trouble for something.

We had no dad around to chastise us, and I think we pushed poor Mum so near to the edge I'm surprised she didn't fall over it. On one occasion it nearly cost Sally her life. Our gang didn't let girls in. Sid would never allow it. As much as Sally begged, pleaded, offered to do the chores, she was never allowed to join. We were always looking for something to amuse us. At the back of the house we found an old pram. Harry, who wanted to be an engineer, said, "Let's make a racing cart."

Micky detached the wheels from the bottom of the pram, just leaving the chassis. We found a box and attached this to the frame across two bits of old wood. Then with a rope, attached it to the wheels in the belief we would be able to steer it down Blackheath Hill which was almost vertical. The further down you got the steeper it became. Micky was first to make the attempt. It was hazardous conditions. There was a layer of surface water where it had been raining, making the road slippery and very dangerous. We pushed him off from the top of the hill and the cart hydroplaned down, flying at high speed; the pram tyres hardly touched the road as it bounced up and down on its hellraising journey. With no brakes and unable to steer, we all thought it was a death-defying feat of bravery.

Micky arrived safely at the bottom much to everyone's surprise and whoops of delight. Sally had been following us around all morning. The boys found her extremely irritating. I, however, enjoyed Sally's company, although she could be very inquisitive and constantly asked questions which could be very tiresome. Sally desperately wanted to join our gang. Sid said if she went down the hill in the cart he would consider letting her. I didn't think this was a very good idea, all I received for my opinion was a kick on the shin. Sally was keen to show the boys how brave she was.

As I helped her into the box, I had an awful premonition. She had a look of utter fear on her face, which I will never forget. Before Sally could change her mind, Sid, Micky, and Harry gave one almighty shove, propelling her down the hill at high speed. We watched the cart for all of one minute before it hit a piece of rubble that we'd failed to notice and remove from our race track. Spinning out of control, it tipped upside down, rolling over and over in its wild descent, throwing Sally high into the air only to smash onto the hard concrete with an impact of such force that she looked like she had been projected from a catapult. Finally, the cart reached its destination and broke into pieces; only the wheels could be seen running away into the distance.

Sally lay still and unmoving on the wet tarmac, her crumpled fragile little body covered in dirt. Blood seeped from her nose which looked as if it was broken.

I said, "You've killed her, Sid. You've killed her." With the picture of Sally's lifeless body in my mind I ran as fast as I possibly could to get me mum. "Sid's killed Sally," I said to me mum when I found her in the kitchen.

"Oh God, not my baby."

Mum took me by the hand, grabbed an old blanket which was hanging over the banisters in the hall and we ran to find Sally. By the time we arrived back at the scene, there was a crowd of unwanted gatherers all trying to be helpful. The boys were now sobbing uncontrollably. By this time, Sally, much to everyone's relief, had started to wake up as if from a deep sleep. We covered her in the blanket. Mrs Taylor from up the road had already called the ambulance from the phone box on the corner of the street. In the distance, I could hear the sound of the ambulance bell letting us know it was on its way, the sound of the bell getting louder and louder as it approached. Sally remained in hospital for two weeks. She had broken her arm, fractured her skull, and had to have three teeth removed. Because of her extreme bravery we awarded her a gold cross. This was an old bit of costume jewellery that Harry found in his mum's bedroom drawer. Sally wore this with pride until she started work at sixteen. We made her an honorary member of our gang much to Sid's objections, and he left shortly afterwards. Me mum sent Sid to live with me dad for a little while to see if a bit of discipline would knock some sense into him. Phyllis, however, was not very happy and it wasn't long before he returned home. I was not allowed out for quite some time and had to clean the outside toilet for a good few months. Sally was none the worse for her escapade. She still loved and trusted Sid and me unconditionally.

Old Chum became very slow and could no longer make the paper round with me. Chum had grown old without us even noticing. Time had just slipped by. She had developed a bad cough and had started to go off her food; she took to sitting alone in the backyard just laying quietly in the sun. I came home from school one day and Mum told me not to get upset but that Chum had died in her sleep. We carried her in the newspaper that mum had bought the fish and chips home in. Then we laid her very gently inside the hole and covered her with earth, just as if we were putting her to bed and wrapping her with a blanket. The three of us stood holding hands. Mum said, "Goodnight Chum, sleep tight." Sally sang the lullaby, 'Rock A Bye Baby' and placed a bunch of wild daisies on her grave. We all cried, even mum wiped a tear away, although she'd never had much time for her really. Sid never bothered to say goodbye or visit the grave. He just said, "We were well rid of the smelly old mongrel."

Chum left a gaping hole in my life and I felt that I had lost my best friend. We never got another dog, Mum said they cost too much money. I missed Chum for a long time. That was my first experience of losing something I really cared for. Sally was the only one who seemed to understand so we became quite close. She would always wait to walk home from school with me and even came with me in the morning to help deliver the papers. Although this stopped when the weather was bad, she preferred to stay in bed. After the incident of the racing cart, Sid and I tried to keep in Mam's good books.

Sid hated living with me dad. He was very strict

with Sid and imposed a curfew on him. He had to report to Phyllis or Dad at all times. This was against all of Sid's principles. Neither of us got on very well with Phyllis; she was very jealous and didn't like Dad spending any time or money on us. Sally, however, she tolerated – even liked. You couldn't not be fond of Sally with her happy and caring nature. Dad decided that we would have to earn our pocket money in future as we were now growing up, and he said we had to be taught life's basic principles. Those were one, hard work, and two, money. Mum said, "Life's two basic principles were love and laugher." And I must say, as the years passed I tended to agree with her.

Aunty Maureen, Dad's half-sister, was very well off and needed a cleaner. So for two hours every morning in the school holidays, Sid and I would go round to her very impressive house situated in one of the posher roads in Blackheath. The house stood on its own at the top of Blackheath Hill; it was very grand and had imposing entrance gates which were tremendous fun to swing backwards and forwards on. If we were found doing so Auntie Maureen would give us a sharp clip round the ear. Sid eventually pulled them off their hinges and put the blame on me. My pocket money was docked for quite a few weeks. Sid never admitted to his part in their destruction.

When we arrived we were given aprons to put on. I would then sit at the old mahogany polished wood table, in the middle of a very imposing dining room. The floor was covered in dark parquet flooring and Sid and I were always made to take our boots off to stop getting mud on the floor. When Mum knew we were going to visit Auntie Maureen she always made sure we wore socks with no holes in. We had to keep up appearances to Dad's side of the family. Aunty Maureen would cover the table with old newspaper. Then, would fetch all the brass and silverware for us to polish. She would instruct us in the art of cleaning, I never knew anyone could have so much silver cutlery and she was never happy till it sparkled and looked like it was fit to be used at a royal banquet. She had been a silver service waitress before she'd married Uncle Cecil so was very fussy, always pretending to be posher than she really was. Me mum used to say, "You've forgotten your roots, Maureen. Never forget where you come from."

Sid and I never really understood, because Auntie Maureen never dyed her hair like she did. Uncle Cecil was a strange man. Very rounded, bald headed with a very long drooping moustache. Food would catch in it when he ate. It used to put Sid and me off our sandwiches. Sid said he kept a spare meal in it for later. His clothes never seemed to fit and he constantly pinched me mum on the bottom when she visited. In the end, she decided to stop going there. Mum said she didn't see why Aunty Maureen had ever married him, but then again, love moves in mysterious ways and there was none so queer as folk.

Sid and I would take it in turns to do the brass. At the end of the two weeks there would be a little white envelope, one for Sid and one for me. Sid spent most of his two hours looking at pictures of naked women that he'd come across accidentally in a book that he'd found hidden in the library. He called them very educational and said they were for medical purposes. When I took a peek, all I saw was pictures of large robust naked ladies in very exotic positions, so they didn't look like medical books to me. Sid said they belonged to Uncle Cecil, Maureen's husband, but he worked on the newspapers, so I didn't understand why he had medical books.

Sid said not to mention the pictures to Aunty Maureen. Why I opened Sid's envelope that morning, I will never know. When I did, I could not believe it. In mine were just brass pennies, in his there were silver coins. I was doing all the work and Sid was being paid for it. I told me dad about the money and the naked pictures. It turned out that Uncle Cecil was putting a few extra coins in Sid's envelope, so that he didn't tell me Aunty Maureen about the pictures he had found in the library. Dad had a few strong words with Uncle Cecil and me mum didn't speak to Aunty Maureen for a considerable time after. They fell out over her telling Uncle Cecil that he was a disgraceful pervert keeping such pictures in the house and he should be ashamed of himself. We didn't go back and clean the brass anymore. Instead Dad took us down the car lot, and we helped vacuum out the cars and polish them ready to be sold. Later on, we learnt Uncle Cecil had been put in prison. We never found out why. Sid said it was cos he'd been found soliciting prostitutes. We were told never to talk about it, being as it was too upsetting, Maureen being Dad's half-sister and all that.

Chapter 13

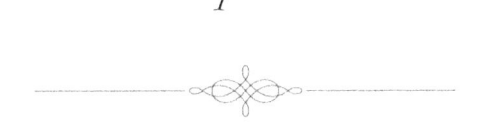

There was always talk about politics in me dad's house. Him and Phyllis would sit and have lots of serious discussions, about Germany and the impending war. I didn't really understand what war meant, but Sid would have great pleasure in showing me how he would fight the Germans, pinning me to the floor with a broom handle that he pretended was a bayonet. War was declared in 1939. It was to last six long years. Mum had pulled the chairs round the radio and gave us a sticky bun each to keep the three of us from fidgeting. I remember it like it was yesterday. It was the last cake we would have for quite a while. Two of the neighbours came in from up the road, as well as uncle Jimmy who used to work for Dad. He was a handsome man, better looking than me dad, me mum said. He was short with blond, thick, curly hair, stocky, and had been a boxing champion for the school when younger so he knew how to look after himself should the need ever arise. His eyes crinkled when he smiled and he laughed a lot, unlike me dad.

Sid and I noticed he seemed to be around rather a lot. Mum grinned at him all the time and would laugh at his silly jokes that neither Sid or I found funny. He'd given up working with Dad and had his own printing company. Me mum and Jimmy were snuggled closely together on the old brown sofa listening to the important news. Neville Chamberlain, the Prime Minister, was making an announcement to the nation. The Germans had failed to withdraw their troops from Poland and consequently we were at war with Germany. The radio crackled intermittently and Uncle Jimmy had to keep tuning it in so we could all hear. Mum and Mrs Bird from up the road cried. Sid whooped and said, "Will I get a gun? I bet there'll be loads of bombs."

Jimmy turned to mum and said, "I'll be expected to sign up, luv." Mum cried.

Dad came round the next day and that was the first time I'd seen Dad and me mum cuddle in years. Dad had said thank God we were too young to sign up. "That's one thing they wouldn't have to worry about."

Dad never went to war. He went for the medical. They found he had a slight heart murmur, so that meant they didn't accept him for active duty. I think he was relieved really, but he wouldn't let on. Dad and Jimmy built an air raid shelter in the back yard. Mum laughed at it, and said we'd all be a lot safer under the stairs. It was 1940 when the heavy bombing started. You could see the glow on the skyline from the fires where the docks had been hit time after time in heavy bombing raids. Houses and shops disappeared, here one day, overnight gone. Food became scarce. Petrol was controlled and difficult to get. Butter and sugar were the first to be rationed. Cheese, tea, jam, and biscuits followed shortly afterwards, and it was almost impossible to get a nice joint of meat.

We all had ration books. They were all different colours. Mine, Sid's and Sally's were blue and me mam's was a sort of buff colour. We had to register our books with 'Micky Darling' as me mum used to call him, from the shop up the road. That's where nearly all our groceries came from. Mum would put on her lipstick, and used to talk to Micky in her sexiest voice in the hope she'd get a good cut of meat. I don't think his real name was darling, cos he didn't half give Sid a funny look when he went to pick up our rations one day, when Mum was unwell and he called Micky, "Darling."

We had to queue for hours sometimes to get the rations. We would take it in turns. Sid never seemed to be around when it was his turn and I was always sent in his place. I loved to listen to all the local gossip and always had to relate it back to her when I got home. The talk was always about the war, when it would end, whose son hadn't come home, who'd got wounded, and who was sleeping with who. It made the time go very quickly, but half of it I couldn't recall by the time I got home, much to me mum's annoyance. Sid, me, and Sally still had our school dinners, so we never went hungry, even if we went without chocolate or sweets. Sometimes we had a bar of chocolate that Uncle Jimmy had managed to get hold of and it would be shared between us. Sid would roll on the floor in ecstasy at the taste of it and we would all pretend to laugh at him.

Uncle Jimmy had a good business running. He took over the local black market. Mum said, "He looked quite the spiv in his striped suit and trilby hat." He always had a suitcase full of cigarettes or nylons, did Jimmy. He used to get them direct from the depot at the docks where he had a contact. Me mum was always frightened he'd be put in prison, but she never said no to a pair of nylons. We seemed to live on corned beef. Mum became very inventive in ways to serve it. After the war finished I could never eat another tin ever again. We were made to eat everything on our plates, Mum would get very cross if we didn't. Her favourite saying was, "Waste not want not."

We were by no means rich, but with Uncle Jimmy's generous gifts we always seemed to manage. He was always bringing something home. We'd always have a bit of cheese or a few biscuits. I think Mum was fond of Jimmy but he wasn't the marrying kind and at time she was still married to me dad. I think she always hoped they'd get back together but that just wasn't to be, much to our disappointment. Mum would have taken him back any time. She said, "You have to forgive and forget, because you never know what the future is going to turn up." We looked on Uncle Jimmy as a father figure when Dad wasn't around. We learnt never to cross him, though. He had a very quick right hand picked up from his boxing days.

It was mid-November; firework night had been suspended because of the blackouts. Sid though, had decided we would have our own fireworks display. Our friend Pete lived on the top of Blackheath Hill. The house was old and Edwardian and to us it always seemed quite dark and foreboding so we didn't go there very often. Pete's parents were very intellectual and if we encountered them on one of our visits it would become a very boring experience so we went there as little as possible, always choosing to meet Pete elsewhere. Pete, on this occasion had told us they would be out. So we all traipsed round, just as it had begun to get dark. We were so excited.

Pete's garden was very long, with a low wall at the end. It backed onto the main road and had a panoramic view over Greenwich Park. Sid said it would be a great place to let off the fireworks that he had managed to get hold of. Where they came from, nobody knew and Sid refused to say. Pete's mum and dad had gone to a violin concert and weren't going to be back until after midnight, so we had plenty of time to have a smoke and help ourselves craftily to a beer from Pete's dad's secret stash, that he thought he had got well hidden. After sharing a beer between us we went into the garden. It was pitch black and if we stood on the wall at the end of the garden we could see the lights from Blackheath village. It looked almost magical as the passing cars going up and down the hill flashed past causing a burst of illumination to hit the garden, enabling us to see what we were doing.

We only had three fireworks, a Catherine wheel and two rockets. The sparklers had just fizzled out after a few weak sparks which had come to nothing. The Catherine wheel we set off first, it rotated violently in a frenzy of colour, reds, greens, and blues, giving us a moment of sheer excitement at the whirling, swishing sound it made as it spun round, creating a whizzing circle of colour. It lasted all of two minutes then sadly died. Sid then took the two rockets, put them into milk bottles, lit them with Uncle Jimmy's cigarette lighter which he had borrowed earlier, hoping that it would not be missed. The first rocket sped on its journey like a space capsule entering orbit out of control. The firework then shot high into the sky but only a flicker of a flame and a few sparks like little bursts of lightening could be seen coming from the missile. The firework then did a double somersault and turned back on itself, falling to earth like a shooting star, zigzagging violently on its descent into the garden, chasing Sid, Pete, and me as if it were a bullet looking for a target. We laughed hysterically, jumping up and down to avoid it, running round the garden pushing one another determinedly out of the way in a desperate attempt not to be hit by the speeding rocket in its energetic pursuit. It eventually came to rest on Pete's foot. It was lucky for him that day he was wearing a good pair of thick-soled boots and not wellingtons.

The firework burnt right through the leather. Pete had a hard job explaining to his mum and dad exactly how it had happened.

In our excitement, the launching of the second rocket had gone unnoticed. Thinking it had just run its course and disappeared we returned home, me mum none the wiser at what we'd been up to. The following morning Mum was waiting in the queue with our ration books. The shop was very late opening. Poor Micky Darling had been driving up Blackheath Hill on his way home from the shop. A firework had gone right through the window screen of his car. He had swerved right. off the road and gone into the bus shelter where you caught the Number 52 into Lewisham. He wasn't hurt luckily, but the car was a complete write-off. We all acted surprised and shocked; Uncle Jimmy asked Sid for his lighter back with the knowing look of a fellow conspirator. Jimmy never said anything to Mum and we kept the secret of the fireworks between us right up until Sid and I left home.

Chapter 14

Uncle Jimmy became a fixture around the house; me mum liked having him around. We were never sure why he didn't enlist. Mum said he had friends in high places. Sid was always a little jealous of Jimmy. He had always been the one who looked after things after Dad left. He didn't take kindly to being told what to do and what time to be in. Jimmy, however, always looked out for me. Just as if I was his own son. I was little for my age and always used to get picked on in school, especially as I used to have to wear Sid's hand-me-downs. They were too big for me, the boots especially, and I had to shove cardboard down the front of them to make them fit. There was one particular bunch of boys that used to try and catch me on the way home from school. There were four of them. Their leader was a large fat boy called Joe Carter. The two Benson brothers and slimy Duck

Henderson made up the rest of the gang. He was called that because he waddled as he walked. I was little, but fast, and could normally outrun them. Today, however, mum had given me a pair of Sid's old school boots to wear. They were enormous and made my feet look very big. In my hurry to dress for school that morning I had forgotten to stuff the toes with cardboard, As I ran they slipped backwards and forwards no matter how hard I tried to grip them on with my toes, slowing me down so I couldn't outrun my pursuers.

Joe Carter was the first to reach me. Why I had become their target I don't know, but they seemed relentless. Feeling a large punch hit me between the shoulder blades, I hit the floor, smacking my nose on the pavement and I could taste the blood as it filled the inside of my mouth, biting my tongue nearly all the way through in the process. Determined not to cry, I endured their violent onslaught of kicks and punches until they decided they'd had enough. Sid had seen what was happening and had just crossed the road. From that moment on a war festered between us. I never could forgive him and found it very hard to call him my brother again. My shirt was torn and covered in blood, my trousers ripped, my lip was split, and my nose broken. Mum was horrified.

She told me off for fighting and yelled at me for the state of my clothes. She was more worried how she could afford new ones. Uncle Jimmy took one look at my face and said, "I'm going to teach you how to box, Bob."

That Saturday I had my first lesson. Uncle Jimmy found a pair of old leather boxing gloves, he'd kept them from his championship days. He fetched round all his old photos, his winning gold belt, and a cup that his old mum kept on her mantelpiece. "We'll make a boxer out of you yet, Bob. You're light on your feet, and you're fast. All we've got to do is teach you how to pack a punch, a mean punch."

Mum didn't think it was such a grand idea, and could see trouble ahead, but she went along with Uncle Jimmy anyways. Every evening after supper, that is if it wasn't raining, Uncle Jimmy would give me a lesson. We were banned from the parlour when Jimmy punched me accidentally too hard on the chin and I fell back, grabbed the tablecloth to save myself from falling and the whole thing slipped off, taking me mum's best vase with it. When it hit the stone floor it broke into thousands of little pieces. As hard as me and Uncle Jimmy tried it never looked the same when he'd stuck it back together, and always leaked if you put flowers in it. It was eventually retired. From that moment on the back yard became the boxing arena. Uncle Jimmy thought I had a talent. He said I should apply to the school boxing team, so that I could be trained in a proper gym. For the time being, I was happy to keep my boxing talent under wraps. That was until Duck Henderson caught me smoking behind the school toilets and said he was going to tell on me. I couldn't have me mum find out I'd been smoking, so I put me fists up on guard and said, "No you won't, Henderson," and packed the biggest punch I had in me. He was a tall boy and I just caught the edge of his face as I swung my fist at him. He just smiled at me and rubbed his chin, and with that punched me squarely on the jaw, knocking me back hard against the toilet door. At that moment it entered my head that perhaps boxing was not such a good idea after all.

The school dinner bell was ringing to signify the end of the lunch break and Mr Johnson, our school teacher, had come to find us. He took one look at us, and said, "You want to fight, boys, you can do it properly in the ring," and with that, he marched us back into the school building and issued us both with a week's worth of detention.

School boxing club was held on Tuesday nights after lessons finished. The gym was transformed into a boxing ring. An old punch bag that had been donated by an ex-pupil was hung from a large hook in the ceiling, and we'd take it in turns to hit it with great vigour. I used to pretend it was fat Joe Carter and punched it repeatedly very hard. Sometimes it would swing back on me and knock me right over, much to everyone's amusement. Part of the sports hall was roped off to give the appearance of a real boxing ring. The deputy headmaster, Mr Castle, would act as referee, and two boys would be allowed to spar with each other under his watchful eye. Mr Johnson, the sports teacher, who ran the club, thought I showed great promise. I could duck and dive very quickly. I'd learnt this from an early age trying to stay out of the way of Sid's flying fists.

The local schools used to hold boxing competitions. There used to be junior and senior sections. The prize was usually a sash and a silver cup which if you won your name would be engraved on it and your photo would be taken and put in the hall of fame along the school corridor. After a few months of training, Mr Johnson said I was ready to represent the school in the junior boxing competition against Blackheath High. I must say, I wasn't really looking forward to it. Getting punched every night was losing its appeal, I was forever sporting a bloody nose or a black eye. I was beginning to think I preferred repairing cars with me dad. It seemed a far safer option.

On the day of the competition, Mum, Jimmy, Sid, and me dad all came to watch. I was really nervous, especially when I saw the size of the lad I was supposed to fight. He was called Jo Skinner, a slimy-looking lad who didn't look like no junior to me. He towered above me and made grimacing faces, and said he was going to beat me to a pulp. When the bell rang, he came at me like a rabid dog. Two minutes into the fight I could feel that my two front teeth had gone through my bottom lip, my nose was bleeding and I was slowly losing the vision in my left eye where it had been constantly punched. I thought, *I've had enough of this,* so with the very next strike I purposefully fell to the floor and closed my eyes very tightly, pretending to be knocked out. I didn't move a muscle praying, they would stop the fight while I still had some dignity. I heard the referee counting down from ten, and thankfully he declared the match over.

Jo Skinner walked round the ring with boxing glove raised high, acknowledging the fact that he had just become the junior boxing champion. Everybody cheered except Mum and Jimmy. He was so disappointed. Sid, he just laughed at me said I had no guts. When I felt it was safe and the fight was officially over, I opened my eyes and let the referee help me up from the floor. Me mum agreed with Uncle Jimmy; much to my relief they came to the conclusion I'd never make a fighter, so they decided that boxing wasn't for me, so I never went back to the after-school boxing club. At least Joe Carter and his gang left me alone after that. Dad was a tad disappointed. Uncle Jimmy said perhaps I'd make a better car mechanic.

I heard later on that Sid had given the Carter gang a good hiding. He never told me, and after their apparent confrontation with him the gang stayed well away from the whole family and never bothered me again, Sid's reputation having gone before.

I was destined to be a car dealer like me dad. Mum said I didn't have a violent bone in my body. Sid was the one always fighting and always in trouble. Mum was always in tears over something he'd done or someone he'd hit, or something he'd stolen. Or someone's daughter he'd frightened. Dad lost control of him. He said Sid had no soul and had been born without a heart. Sally used to say his soul was just lost and we needed to help him find it. Uncle Jimmy said, his soul had walked too far up the wrong path and no one would find it now. Mum used to cry when he said things like that. I used to laugh, all I could see was a bit of old fish walking up the road with Sid chasing it, calling after it, saying, "Come back. I've lost you."

I think Mum was falling in love a bit. Uncle Jimmy had such a good heart. He used to make her laugh. Dad, I think, was always jealous, and although he liked Jimmy, there was always tension when he was around. Mum used to play one off against the other. It used to drive them both mad. When Dad lost his temper with Sid they nearly always ended up raising their fists at each other. If it had not been for Uncle Jimmy getting in between them, I dread to think what the outcome might have been. I used to disappear at any sign of trouble and keep my head down. That is until Sally would give me the all clear. It used to upset Sally, all the rows. She was always the peacemaker in the house, but Sid never really took notice of anyone. He was a law unto himself. No one really understood why Sid was unbalanced. It was sad really, because he was given no help at all.

In those days there was no help for boys like Sid. Dad used to worry about him. He thought he was becoming dangerous. Especially when he beat the two Skinner brothers to a pulp. That was to be the start of his downfall.

Sometimes bombs which were intended for the

docks found their way to Blackheath, Lewisham, and Greenwich. Prefabs were put up on the Heath to house the poor families that had lost everything. They certainly weren't a pretty sight but they were meant to be a short-term provision to help with the shortage of housing. We were lucky enough not to suffer any damage from the bombs and our house remained intact all the way through the war, although there were a couple of very near misses. Mum kept her job at the Roxy cinema, but even that suffered and had to be evacuated several times, much to people's annoyance, because they never got to see the end of the film.

Sid and I used to get the tram when Mum was working and go and visit Dad. They were noisy smelly things and swayed from side to side and made me feel sick. Sid used to hang off the back and jump off before paying. He would leave me on board and I wouldn't know which stop to get off at. I couldn't remember how to get to Dad's and quite often got lost and had to return home without seeing him. Sid would always tell Dad that I hadn't wanted to come. He would collect my pocket money as well as his. The only money I had was my earnings from doing odd jobs. One time Sid got caught out; when he jumped off the tram without paying Dad was driving behind.

We both got marched back to Mum and had our pocket money docked. Dad wasn't that cross with us though, because he'd done the same thing when he was a boy. He told mum that he would come to pick us up for future visits. That way Mum would always know we'd arrived there safely.

Later on, Dad joined the home guard. He said he wanted to do his bit. He had an old air rifle that he carried which made him feel important. He learnt a few German phrases and Sid and I used to laugh at his strange accent. Dad said he was the extra eyes and ears of the military and he was always on the lookout for spies. Of a night, he'd go on patrol and check people's identity cards. They didn't pay him a wage though and it was all voluntary so Dad still took in cars for repair. Although because of the petrol rationing these were few and far between. Money became short. Food became scarce, the threat from the bombs more frequent; school became a hit-and-miss affair and much to Sid's delight because he hated school, he was allowed to join Uncle Jimmy selling things out of suitcases on the black market. The government decided that we were in danger from the bombings which often destroyed schools as well as residential houses so they decided to evacuate us children to protect us from the air raids. So, it was agreed by me mum and dad that Sid, me, and Sally would be sent off to a safer location in the country. We were each allocated a gas mask and me mum was told to pack us two vests, two pairs of pants, a pair of trousers each, six clean handkerchiefs, and a warm jersey. Sally was to also have two pairs of stockings, a petticoat, a blouse, and a warm cardigan. We each had an overcoat, a pair of good Sunday shoes and boots, and we all went off to the station. We were each given a paper bag filled with big black juicy cherries. Although Mum and Dad were not being forced to send us they felt it would be safer.

Chapter 15

Bert's life changed forever the day Connie walked into the coffee shop in Blackheath. He hadn't meant to hurt her. Phyllis, well, she was his bit of fun, his light relief from all the stress of having to deal with Sid every day. Connie, well, she was different, he really loved her. Phyllis, well, well she was more of a good time girl. She wanted all the benefits of a man but she would say, "Not the washing and ironing." That came with them. Benefits, meaning the sex, the meals out, the presents, and certainly not the babies.

That was lucky really, Bert thought to himself, because he'd got the mumps off one of little Bob's friends which had rendered him impotent. The doctor had told him that he couldn't father any more kids after Sally. He never told Phyllis it was his fault that there were no babies. It was for the best really. He certainly didn't want to have another Sid. He'd always said to Connie that he'd was a mixed blessing, that boy, and there was something wrong with him and a screw was loose right from birth. The night he'd turned up at Phyllis's with his suitcase, he thought she was going to turn him away. Phyllis hadn't really thought it was a permanent thing between the two of them. Connie was her best friend, after all. That night had turned into two and then three. He'd not even realised that Connie had been pregnant with Sally when he had left. He should have returned home when Sally was born. He'd tried, but Connie would have none of it. Couldn't and wouldn't forgive. Proud, and independent, that's what he loved about her.

Maybe not quite as good at the sex bit, but that's why him and Phyllis had hit it off so well. She was like an untamed tiger. He had the scratches to prove it. The car lot – he called it his empire to everyone – had started to struggle and what with all the talk of war, he found it very difficult keeping two homes going. Phyllis expected the world. She always wanted the best of everything. "None of these copies off the market," she would say to Bert. "I'm not Connie, you know. Can't put up with second best." Bert knew she was talking about Jimmy. There was always that element of jealousy between her and Connie over Jimmy. He was one of Phyllis's ex boyfriends. He'd blown Phyllis out. Jimmy had told Connie that Phyllis had been too expensive to keep going and he didn't have enough gas in the tank and he'd run out of petrol. That used to make me mum really giggle, thinking of Phyllis as an old banger. That's what we all used to call her behind her back.

When war broke out Bert had tried to enlist. The recruitment office had turned him down. He was devastated. They told him he had a heart murmur. He thought his heart was probably broken because Connie never would take him back. In the end, he'd just stopped trying. Jimmy got on well with the boys and even handled Sid better than he did without losing his temper, so he'd just let things tick on. With the war came his own problems, he'd become a Home Guard and wasn't it his duty to protect? Hadn't he always fancied himself as a secret agent, suave and sophisticated doing one's bit for one's Queen and country? Every night Bert and one of his mates would patrol the streets. "Keeping everyone safe!" That's what Dad would say. Bert loved the feeling of importance it gave him; the way people would tip their hats to him in an acknowledgement of respect for what he was doing. As a car salesman, no one had any regard for you at all. In fact, they always thought you were a cheat and a lowlife always ready to sell you a car that was overpriced and never fit for purpose. In fact, in some people's eyes it was almost as bad as being a money lender, but it paid the bills.

It was a bitterly cold evening and Phyllis had made him wear a thick woollen scarf that she had knitted for him. He thought it made him look like a clown. It was bright red in colour and he felt stupid as Bill kept taking the rise out of him by saying it was as red as his face. He was glad of it now. It was keeping the cold out and as they walked along the street they discussed tactics on what they would do if they were ever to meet a German spy. The air raid warning came loud and clear, echoing through the empty streets. Bert and Bill knew it was to be the start of a very long night. Bill was not to know it was to be his last. Bert hoped Connie had got the three children with her and was taking them down to the shelter that he and Jimmy had attempted to build in the back yard with the Home Office guidelines.

Within twenty minutes the first bomb had fallen, finding its target. You could smell the feeling of panic and desperation around as the world erupted into complete chaos. Number 62, Albemarle Road had taken a direct hit. Half of the house had tumbled like a pack of cards when the German bomb struck. As Bert and Bill turned the next corner they could see and hear the desperate cries of a mother whose children were somewhere underneath the rubble, in what was left of the once loved family home. At that moment, Bert decided his kids would have to be sent away and he would have to somehow persuade Connie to evacuate them to a place of safety as far away from the bombing as they could go. Bill and Bert walked purposely towards the young woman who was now on her knees scrabbling frantically in the dirt. The shell of the house which looked like an old monumental historical ruin was shaking precariously and looking like it would teeter and fall any minute on top of the band of rescuers who were trying to reach the children.

"Clear the way," Bert said. "Home Guard, stand clear." With that, he removed his scarf, handed it to Bill and ventured nervously into what was the remains of the bombed out building. In the distance the sounds of the ambulance bells could be heard racing through the streets to get to them. Bert reached the frightened boy first and handed him quickly out to Bill, who in turn handed him to his relieved and grateful mother who was sobbing loudly. They could hear the cries of the little girl who was still alive. When she'd heard the air raid warning, thinking there was not enough time to get to the safety of the shelter, she had run down to the cellar, and now lay wedged underneath a large concrete slab, unable to move under the weight of the fallen debris. The entrance down to the cellar was completely blocked except for a tiny gap just big enough for a slightly built person to crawl through. Bill, being younger and slimmer, squeezed his way through the gap which had once been the doorway that led down the stairs to where the little girl lay injured. He was still clutching Bert's scarf with the intention of wrapping it round the child.

Without any prior warning, just like somebody had taken a deep breath and blown outwards, creating a violent and destructive tunnel of twirling air, what was left of the house fell to the ground, creating a cloud of thick white dust that flew everywhere. It choked your lungs and burnt the back of your throat, leaving your nose blocked and unable to breathe freely. That was the last thing Bert remembered.

Phyllis was awoken the following morning with a knock on the door. There were two policemen standing outside looking very solemn. In their hands they were holding the red scarf that she had given Bert to wear that night. They informed her that Bert had died a brave hero. He had been clutching the red scarf when they had pulled him and the little girl, dead, from the rubble. Phyllis walked into the kitchen, before sitting down she took a bottle of sherry brandy from the cupboard and poured herself a very large glass and drank it as if it were a glass of orange. Then repeated over and over again. "Not my Bert. Not my Bert." Phyllis then went into the bedroom climbed into bed and pulled the covers up around her for comfort and fell into a deep, drink-induced sleep, woken up a few hours later by Bert pulling her towards him. He was covered in white dust, speaking with a strange deep, croaking voice that she didn't recognise, thinking he was a ghost, or maybe even a zombie. She was unable to open her eyes. To petrified to look at the image that stood there waving its arms dramatically in their attempt to get her attention and for her to acknowledge its presence. It took Phyllis quite a while before she recovered from the experience.

Bert had been taken away by ambulance to hospital; he'd been knocked unconscious, not coming round for several hours. It was Bill who had died trying to save the child. When the body was recovered from the rubble it was identified by George, another member of the Guards. Before Bert had gone on patrol, George told him how lucky he was to have someone knit a scarf like that for him. He had no idea that Bert had passed the scarf to Bill, who had been clutching it when the building had collapsed on top of him. When George saw the scarf he recognised it as Bert's and presumed the body that he identified that night to be his. If he had been braver and looked a little closer, he would have realised it was Bill lying dead, the two men being significantly different from each other in build.

Phyllis never really forgave George for the unfortunate mistake. Being told Bert was dead and then the shock of seeing his ghost at the end of her bed. It was a long time before she drank anything with alcohol in it and could never tolerate the smell of Sherry Brandy, let alone drink one. It reminded her too much of the terrible incident. Phyllis gave up knitting and took up baking instead. There was always an abundance of uneatable hard rock cakes. Sid and I would challenge each other to munch our way through one of her indigestible attempts at cooking. We always tried hard to look as if we were enjoying it for fear of upsetting her. On one of our visits to dad's, Sid lost a tooth, which later was found imbedded in the remains of a cake that half eaten and abandoned had fallen down the back of the sofa, that not even the cat had thought worth eating.

Bert never had the heart to wear the scarf again it was placed over the coffin at Bill's funeral . What a grand send off he had. Black coach and horses. Their feathered plumes flying proudly as they clip clopped along the street carrying Bill to the crematorium and back home to his final sentry post. Bill's children tried to be very grown up; they gave a lovely eulogy saying how their dad had been so brave carrying out his duty and how proud they were of him. Bert sat in the church that day thinking, *There for the grace of God go I*. And putting his hands together in prayer, he gave a simple thank you that it was Bill that died that day, and not him. Always being very careful to avoid dangerous situations, always thinking of his responsibility to his own family.

Chapter 16

Mum finally, after many objections, agreed it was best for us to be evacuated. So, all the arrangements were duly made, and we were all packed ready. Dad took us to Blackheath Railway Station, me mum said goodbye to us at home. She was too upset to see us get on the train. Sid, me, and Sally each had had a label attached to our coats, but neither one of us knew where we were going. A posh-looking lady took Sally by the hand. I tried to hang on to her but her hand was prised firmly out of mine and I watched her disappear into the crowd along the platform. I could hear her sobbing loudly and she was yelling out mine and Sid's names as she looked back over her shoulder. Sid and I were propelled along the platform and were shoved unceremoniously into the next open train door. We were told to sit down quietly. At that moment, we had the feeling we might never see

Mum, Dad, or Uncle Jimmy ever again. We were uncertain where we were going and we were cold, hungry, and very tired by the time the train pulled into Garndiffaith railway station. It had taken five hours of stopping and starting and picking up other children along the way destined for evacuation to South Wales.

As the train pulled into the station Sid put his head out of the window. Lining the platform were crowds of people that had come to pick one of us evacuees. We dismounted from the carriage, stepping onto the platform, it became quite a free for all as the locals argued between themselves over the stronger and healthier looking boys. We were like a large bag of sweets, each person trying to pick their favourite before it was greedily swallowed by someone else, all wanting the older ones. The smaller younger ones and the girls were left till last. Sid was picked first.

"Here's a good strong boy," I heard someone say.

"The little one looks healthy too," a woman's voice piped up. A thickset, fat, red-faced woman wearing a very dirty apron grabbed me by the arm with one hand and picked up my suitcase in the other. Sid was being marched off some way ahead with a tall, balding, unshaven, scruffy-looking man, who looked like he'd come out of a gangster movie and who spoke with a very strange accent that I could hardly understand. "Wait for me, Evan," she said. "This one's going to take a bit of training." With that she clipped me smartly behind the ears with the back of her hand and told me to hurry up. "The sheep have got to be fetched in yet, and the parlour has to be scrubbed." We then began our four-mile walk to our new home, me sobbing loudly and Sid plodding silently on ahead, trying hard to keep up with the disagreeable Evan who was to be our guardian for the next few years. My feet had already begun to hurt as I was wearing a pair of Sid's old boots. These had a large hole in the sole which Mum had covered with cardboard in an attempt to make them last longer. The water had now seeped in, drenching my socks, and as we walked up the muddy uneven track, which was covered in deep puddles, every stone felt like I was treading on a large boulder.

Already the light was failing and a low mist with the onset of fine drizzle was creeping down the back of my collar. But the chill in my bones was not from the cold, but the uncertainty of what lay ahead.

Chapter 17

Sally was desperately trying to free herself from the unknown woman who was pulling her away from the platform. This was the last glimpse that she would catch of her brothers for a very long time. The tall, elegantly dressed, middle-aged woman was beautifully attired in a Chanel-type tweed suit; on her head sat a brown pillar-box hat which rested at a precarious angle. When she smiled, she looked like she was about to break into peals of laughter. "My name is Mrs Heart," she said to Sally. "Don't be frightened. You are coming to live with me and a few friends in the country. You'll love it," she said. "There's lots of animals for you to play with, and it's very safe, away from all the bombs. Your mother and father can visit."

Sally stopped crying and smiled up at the woman. no longer afraid of what might happen to her, thinking what a lovely name this lady had and how pleasant she was. They trotted hand in hand out of the station where parked at the kerbside was a magnificent car, although Sally had no idea at the time, it was a Rolls Royce Phantom saloon. The door was held open by young man dressed in a very smart chauffeur's uniform. He wore a long grey jacket with an excessive amount of large gold buttons which fastened it tightly together. Black trousers, and a pair of boots that were very highly polished completed the look. Sally thought if she stared at them closely enough she would see her face. Cheekily on his head was perched a peaked hat, that reminded Sally of the conductor from the Number 52 bus that went to Lewisham.

A scruffy little hand appeared out the side of the car. The nails had been chewed down alarmingly short and were etched in dirt and a little silver charm bracelet adorned the wrist. A smiley face followed the hand. "I'm Molly," the blonde, curly-haired little girl said.

Followed by, "I'm David, and this here next to me is Kit, and the quiet one in the corner is Lionel."

Sally squeezed into the back seat beside them. Things didn't seem as bad as she thought after all. Mrs Heart then passed in a big paper bag of boiled sweets for their journey. Closing the door with a slam, she said to Preston the chauffeur, "I'll see you at the house this evening. I'm going to do some shopping. Jeffery will bring me back to the country tonight. Mrs Baxter will settle the children in." The chauffeur climbed into the driver's seat and started the car then turned round to the children to make sure that all the doors were safely shut, opened the car window, tipped his peaked cap at Mrs Heart and slowly pulled away from the kerb. The drive to Ascot in Berkshire where Mr and Mrs Heart lived on their countryside estate was a journey that could be undertaken on a good run in just under two hours, but this day due to the misfortunate circumstances that befell the little band of adventurers which was to be etched on Sally's memory for the rest of her life, took much longer. They were about an hour into their journey, when the accident happened. The young chauffeur had been listening to the radio. He drove along, not paying much attention to the shenanigans that were taking place in the back of the car. The children had been fighting over the last boiled sweet that remained in the paper bag, and were pushing and shoving each other in attempt to grab it from Lionel, who was holding it high above his head. David made a grab for the bag. The car should have ideally only taken four passengers, but had five children squeezed into the back. Lionel was pushed hard against the door. As

David leapt for the bag of sweets, without thinking Lionel grabbed the car door handle which immediately swung open, the children were horrified as he flew from the car, hitting the road so hard the impact must have killed him instantly. As the car motored on, they turned their heads and watched as he rolled over and over, eventually coming to rest in the muddy ditch at the side of the road.

They screamed at the chauffeur to stop the car, who now realizing what had happened slammed his foot hard on the brakes nearly propelling the children into the front seat. Preston climbed out of the car and ran towards Lionel. His eyes were wide open, staring vacantly with an emptiness that Preston knew just by looking into them that the boy was dead, his head hanging loosely, his neck broken. Preston picked the child up very gently and carried him carefully back to the car , covering him tenderly with the picnic blanket he placed him inside the boot closing it with a slam. He knew sadly that it was the last time Lionel would ever travel in a Rolls-Royce or see the blue of the sky or feel the warmth of the sun on his face at least in this lifetime.

The children now reduced to a shocked silence were unable to comprehend what had happened and sat holding each other tightly. In fear that one of them could also disappear never to be seen again. As they continued their journey to Berkshire they could hear Preston quietly crying, every so often he would take a large white handkerchief from his pocket and attempt to wipe away his tears. Lionel was never discussed again. The terrible accident which had caused his death was not mentioned either. It became like a guilty secret never to be disclosed. Two days after they arrived at the house a young couple came to the door and rang the bell. They were shown discreetly into the library. Mrs Heart was heard sharing her deepest sympathies with them. They left shortly afterwards, the gentleman holding the young woman tightly to him. The children watched them, believing that she would have fallen to the ground if her companion had let her go. The couple could be heard weeping loudly as they walked slowly away from the house. Neither of them looked back. The children never saw them again.

Soon forgetting poor Lionel, they settled into the household routine well. They were enrolled in the local village school. This, they attended on weekdays, leaving their weekends for adventurous pursuits in the house. On rain-free days they would venture into the grounds. They discovered an abundance of wildlife, creatures they never knew existed. Coming from a busy built-up area, they had never seen such things as frogs, tadpoles, and dragonflies and each day brought a new and exciting experience for them.

Chapter 18

The house was an adventure waiting to happen. It had fourteen bedrooms, six bathrooms, and long, winding, darkened hallways with ancestral portraits lining the walls. The children would run up and down using them as a running track. Sometimes they would knock over a member of the household staff, or one of the suits of armour which were placed at strategic points along the walkways, these having been worn in great battles by one of the distant warring relatives of Mr and Mrs Heart. This would make Mrs Baxter angry, but she never chastised the children; she had no little ones of her own, and always treated them with great affection. Mrs Baxter was the housekeeper and was employed to keep the servants in check and run the household for Mrs Heart. The two girls, Molly and Sally, had been given a really grand room to sleep in usually reserved for the important guests.

A large carved oak four-poster bed stood in the centre covered with a cream and gold brocade throw and a cluster of large gold cushions scattered elegantly in the middle, each sporting a coat of arms. Draped from the canopy were the sheerest voile curtains which gave the bed an Arabian appearance. Molly and Sally would spend hours pretending to be a royal queen or a princess waiting for their suitor.

David and Kit were put above the stables. Mrs Heart thought it safer if the boys stayed under the watchful eye of the chauffeur and slept in the rooms adjacent to his. At night, they could hear the sound of the horses in the stalls kicking the wooden partitions that separated them from each other, and the whinnying from a young chestnut colt that was waiting to be broken. The two Labradors, which were the estate gun dogs, Jess and Master, slept in the tack room. Sometimes of a night the boys would creep down and take them back up to their room for company.

Breakfast in the house was a grand affair. It was served every morning at 7.30 and it was considered very bad manners to be late. Mr Heart would sit at one end of the long, highly polished walnut table and Mrs Heart the other. The two boys on one side with Molly and Sally sitting opposite them. Breakfast would be laid out on a majestically tall sideboard. The children being so small couldn't reach the food easily and would need assistance from one of the staff to help fill their plates. There were large bowls of cereal, exotic fruit that they had never seen before which must have come from some foreign country and eggs scrambled or fried sometimes poached would be placed under large silver domes. On Sundays there would be kippers or pancakes with syrup. The silver lids were too heavy for the children to lift, and they were embarrassed to ask for help, so they nearly always had cereal as they only helped themselves to what they could reach.

The estate grounds were so vast that the chauffeur used to have to drive them to the small village school where they had been enrolled, as it was too far for them to even walk to the end of the drive. On leaving the house from the rear entrance and entering the main garden, once you had walked through the topiary which had the most amazing mythical creatures and exotic birds fashioned out of the bushes which resembled something out of *Alice in Wonderland*, you would then pass through the kitchen garden and climb over a small wooden style. After a short walk keeping the maze to your left, which had been left unattended for quite some time and the entrance had long since been concealed with wild brambles, you would come upon the boating lake. It was breathtakingly beautiful. Round the edge of the lake floated large patches of green foliage hiding an abundance of hidden aquatic life and on the top skimmed darting dragonflies and tiny frogs jumping amongst the lily pads. The lake was strictly out of bounds and the children had been forbidden to play near it or on it. This, however, to the children, was an open invitation and a disaster waiting to happen.

Molly threw the heavy coverlet off the bed, and swung her legs over the side, stretching them as far as they would go so that she could reach the floor. She was tiny for seven, thin and had a very pale complexion which made her look unwell. Her blonde hair which had now been expertly washed and combed by Mrs Baxter hung in ringleted curls that reached her shoulders. She had a naughty disposition, but a likeable nature and you could not be cross with her for long. Sally seemed to have had a growing spurt, and favouring Dad's side of the family had now caught up with children of the same age. Sally was always the one to take command and took on the role of mother to Kit and David. Molly was a law unto herself, and would often wander on the estate alone, although Mrs Baxter did try and attempt to keep

Molly under her wing and out of trouble.

The first ray of light had started to filter through the small gap in the heavily patterned brocade curtains, and the early morning chatter of the maids could be heard along the corridors as the rest of the house, now awake, had started their daily chores. Mrs Heart's maid tapped on the door to remind the two girls it was nearly seven and breakfast would be served in half an hour. Molly jumped from the bed, but not before throwing a pillow at Sally's head to make sure that she was awake. They dressed together, laughing and giggling as they pulled up their socks, and put on the cotton dresses Mrs Heart had brought them back from London the day before.

They made the two small girls look remarkably like sisters. Molly grabbed Sally's hand. "Don't we look posh," she said. "If only me mum could see me."

They ran down to breakfast, skipping and running.

"You'll be the death of me," Mrs Baxter said when meeting them in the corridor looking at the black fingerprints they were imprinting on the wall, as they pushed each other in their eagerness to get to breakfast. Rubbing the marks off with her best handkerchief, tutting loudly she followed on behind them.

Kit and David had already eaten their breakfast, and Saturday not being a school day, they had gone walking on the estate with the gamekeeper and the two dogs. Mr and Mrs Heart had gone into Ascot, having left much earlier in the car. They had medical issues to deal with, Mrs Baxter had said. "Ladies' problems." They would be gone all morning.

Molly and Sally went into the breakfast room – it was empty. Only the half-eaten bowls of porridge and the remains of a broken bread roll scattered across the table, which Kit and David had thrown at each other in a childish attempt to use the porridge as target practice, left any clues that they had already eaten. Molly and Sally reached as high as they could and managed by standing on their toes to tip up the side of the fruit bowl, so they could grab an apple each. Then stepped out through the French windows onto the patio. The doors had been left ajar by the maid in an attempt to get rid of the smell, which now lingered behind from the charcoaled bacon and the burnt toast which had been presented to Mr Heart earlier. Much to his dismay and annoyance, the new cook was not as experienced as he had first thought.

Molly skipped ahead, taking bites from the large red apple. As the juice ran from the side of her mouth, she wiped her face clean with the pinafore from her new dress. Sally slapped her affectionately. "Don't do that, you'll stain your new frock and Mrs Baxter will be extremely cross with you," she said, as her own apple went into her pocket to eat later. They passed through the topiary, and entered the kitchen garden, Molly forging ahead, Sally running behind in an effort to keep up with her.

The gardener tipped his battered old hat to them. "Morning girls. Come to help me in the garden?"

But Molly's intentions were to get to the wooden gate, and Sally then realised that they were heading for the boating lake, which was completely out of bounds. Before Sally could stop her Molly had pulled the heavy old wooden door open and setting a strong pace, pushed her way through the overgrown brambles and wild flowers until the boating lake came into sight. The lake was about three miles across, surrounded by tall trees, and very deep. Mrs Baxter had told them of giant fish with large teeth that lived in the depths, in the hope that they would stay away from the water. Molly and Sally never really believed her, but there was always that niggling doubt she might be telling them the truth. In the centre of the lake was a small island on which stood a glass summer house. Mrs Baxter said there was a grave on the island and that's where Mrs Heart's baby was buried. She had died of whooping cough and the Hearts had been unable to have any more.

The lake was home to swans, ducks, and wildfowl and there were plenty of places to sit and picnic nicely shaded from the sun. A pathway ran all the way round the lake making it ideal for an afternoon walk. There was an old wooden jetty and in the summer months invited guests would put on a bathing costume and dive into the water to cool off. At the end of the jetty secured by a rusty old chain, the padlock long broken, was a pedal boat. This, Molly was heading for with the sole purpose of visiting the island. Molly ran along the jetty. "Come along, Sally. Hurry up," she said, as she expertly untied the chain and released the little boat from the mooring. It was as if she had done it all her life. Jumping into the boat, she shouted, "Come on, coward. I'll go without you."

Sally, who was unable to swim, shook her head. "No, Molly, we will get into so much trouble if we are found out."

Without looking back Molly placed her feet into the rusty pedals, then as fast as she could, steered the brightly coloured pedal boat which looked like it had come from a fairground towards the island. It rocked from side to side in a dangerous and precarious manner, Sally watching helplessly as the boat skimmed along the water heading for the centre of the lake, Molly screaming in delight at the forbidden adventure she was undertaking with no thought to the risks that could possibly lead to a tragic outcome.

It was springtime and unknown to them, nesting time for the wild swans, making them very territorial and aggressive, the male swans being very protective. The birds have a wingspan of at least seven feet. As Molly neared the island, a giant white mute swan flew across the water; the sound from its vibrant throbbing wings could be heard as it lunged at the boat, flapping its wings repeatedly. It attacked, again and again, striking Molly who was unable to hold on any longer and fell overboard into the water, the swan's giant wings folding over her, trying to push her under. Molly screamed loudly and gripped the side of the pedal boat for all her life's worth, desperately trying not to let the weight of her wet clothes and boots drag her beneath the boat to a certain death. Sally watched helplessly from the bank, unable to go to Molly's aid, powerless as the swan flew in for its final attack. Suddenly she heard a loud shout from behind her, "Get down!"

Sally ducked. She heard a loud bang, and realised that a rifle shot had been fired above her head.

Gasping, she watched as the large white bird fell from the sky, hitting the water with an almighty splash. Its majestic body floated sadly amid the water reeds, amongst which were hidden his three tiny cygnets who were squawking and whistling in their distress. The large male mute swan had sadly given his life to protect his young family as the gamekeeper, hearing Sally's cries, knowing the danger she was in, had shot the bird dead. Molly gripped the side of the boat, crying uncontrollably. The gamekeeper stripped to the waist, dived into the water and pushed Molly and the boat back to the safety of the bank. Sally helped Molly, who was shaking uncontrollably and her teeth were clicking together, making a peculiar chattering noise, onto the bank. Sally thought the noise of her teeth so loud it sounded like a workman drilling the road.

If the young gamekeeper had not been there that day to hear their cries, it would have been a very different outcome to Molly's adventurous game. Molly and Sally were punished accordingly for disobeying the rules. They never went again to the boating lake unsupervised, and from that day on a new padlock was put on the door in the kitchen garden. Molly always hated birds of any kind after that incident, never even feeding the ducks on the village green. Although the three cygnets were taken in by the gamekeeper and hand reared; much to Molly's relief they were released back onto the lake a few weeks later. The dead swan was taken by the gamekeeper to the taxidermist who stuffed and mounted him. He was put in a glass case in the library. It was always a stark reminder to them about the incident. Molly refused to go into the library. She always said the bird's eyes followed her round the room and it gave her nightmares.

The incident of the swan was etched on the children's memory for a long time, but life on the estate was very exciting and the chauffeur and the gamekeeper were always rescuing them from one adventure to another, and it was not long before they were in trouble again and were being rescued or reprimanded for some adventure they had embarked on.

Chapter 19

Sally, Molly, and the two boys settled in well to country routine. It was very different from their lives at home in Blackheath. They went to church on a Sunday in the neighbouring village. The boys were taught to shoot and ride and the girls took piano lessons and elocution. They were taught how to pronounce their vowels and were educated in the art of entertaining and receiving guests. Mum and Dad wrote to Sally regularly, only visiting once. Me mum was very uncomfortable when she was shown into the library and Sally curtsied to her and called her 'Mother'. Molly's mum never came at all. Sally often asked her why. Molly just said her mum wasn't fit to travel; everyone thought it was because she was unwell. Later on, when Molly was told her mother had passed away helping the war effort, Sally heard Mrs Heart telling Mrs Baxter that Molly's mother was a drunk and a prostitute who'd fallen underneath a tram. Mrs Baxter said, "The only effort Molly's mother made for the war effort was to raise a glass." Molly never cried much, she just wondered what would happen to her after the war.

In the school holidays the boys would help the estate manager on the farm. They learnt how to look after the pigs and about animal husbandry. Cook taught the girls how to make scones and bread, and Mrs Baxter showed them how to do needlepoint. Sally and her young companions were oblivious to the damage that was happening in London, and for them life became a long holiday with them growing very fond of Mr and Mrs Heart and calling them Aunty and Uncle.

The war raged on and it wasn't until 1945 that children started to return home to their own families. Molly, however, stayed with Mr and Mrs Heart, who, having grown extremely fond of her, adopted her officially. Molly eventually left them when she married the local teacher at eighteen. Sally returned home a different person and to a different life, finding it very difficult to settle back home with Mum, Blackheath being a lot different from the luxury she had encountered while living with the Hearts. She became quite dissatisfied for a while, but never forgot the valuable grounding and education she received and kept in touch with the Hearts all her life.

Chapter 20

Kit was devastated when his mum Janet had dropped him off at the railway station. He hadn't wanted to go at all. He was a very lonely child, and had a violent father who drank himself to oblivion. Much to his mum's distress, this did not help erase Kit's passion for food. Instead he used it as a comfort which helped ease his pain for the lack of affection he received from his father.

Janet was glad to get him out the way. She was worried he would come to some dreadful harm from his father who was so disagreeable and sometimes violent when he had one too many beers on a Saturday night. On their arrival at Blackheath station, a stern-looking woman wearing a military uniform and carrying a clipboard directed him and his mother towards a group of children. There a shy boy who introduced himself as Lionel and a scruffy, very pale-looking blonde girl called Molly, who didn't look at all well. Alongside her was a smartly dressed boy who was very polite and spoke as if he had his mouth stuffed with sweets. He introduced himself as David. The expensive-looking car stood shining like a minted coin, waiting for them. It was the handsomest car Kit had ever seen and he recognised it immediately as a Rolls Royce. *Wow*, he thought. *I'm going to ride in that*. Suddenly he felt quite light hearted and as he climbed into the back seat, the lady in the military uniform looked inside the car, writing on her clipboard. Room for one more. Then turning her back on them, went inside the station.

Twenty minutes later she returned. The children, now bored, were fidgeting and arguing amongst themselves. Walking alongside her was a very attractive lady wearing a hat that Kit's mother eyed enviously. Holding her hand was a little girl with bright red hair the colour of a carrot. It hung untidily over her shoulders and as she walked towards him the wind blew, causing it to fly in all directions, making her look as if she had been caught in a wind tunnel. She had an exceptionally smiley face, covered in hundreds of freckles. Sally squeezed herself in beside Kit. The chauffeur then closed the door and they went on their way.

An hour into the journey a terrible accident occurred. It all happened so quickly they had been helpless to save Lionel. He would never get to know him now, he'd appeared to have been such a nice boy. Preston the chauffeur told them he'd broken his neck.

Kit had never seen a dead body before and he felt so traumatised by the incident he held Sally's hand for the remainder of the journey in case he to fell out of the car and met the same fate. He looked out of the window, momentarily distracted from his thoughts of poor Lionel, his attention drawn to the Red deer mostly brown in colour with pale spots which could be seen browsing in the surrounding fields. He has only ever seen them in picture books at school. The Stags raised their majestic heads in interest as they heard the car passing, their imposing branched antlers raised upwards giving the animals the appearance they were challenging you. The children were in complete awe of these powerful animals that were running wild.

"Are they dangerous?" Kit asked.

"Only when they are mating," the chauffeur replied.

Finally after what seemed a lifetime the car passed the large wrought iron gates marking the entrance to the estate. The chauffeur slowly manoeuvred the Rolls Royce up the long winding drive through the impressive grounds. Huge oak trees made strange swishing noises as the leaves brushed against the side of the car, their branches over time had grown so long they now shadowed the drive forming a green overhead tunnel which obscured the sun throwing the car into darkness until it emerged the other side into the daylight. Sally said her impression of the house and grounds when she first saw them, was she had been dreaming and had accidentally stepped into a fairytale. The chauffeur told them the trees were hundreds of years old and they had been there long before the house was even built. Eventually the car came to a halt at the resplendent front entrance This was they were going to live and call home for the next few years.

At the bottom of the steps stood the housekeeper and a few of the staff who had been waiting patiently for them to arrive. Mrs Baxter was a grey haired, middle aged woman with a very pleasant manner about her. The chauffeur explained about the accident, she gasped bringing her hand up to her mouth in horror then hurriedly opened the car door and ushered the children into the enormous hallway.

Preston the chauffeur and the gamekeeper William removed Lionel's battered little body from the confinement of the boot. He still felt warm. They thought , although knowing it was impossible that he might wake up and speak. The chauffeur hoping he had made a terrible mistake and Lionel was not dead at all.

He weighed hardly anything. They wrapped the blanket tightly around him to conceal his face so they would not upset the children any further. Preston hoped it would be the only time he would ever be faced with anything quite as heartbreaking and tragic.

He blamed himself for not checking on the children's behaviour and perhaps the pointless accident could have been avoided. He was not sure he could forgive himself today or ever. It was he knew going to haunt him for the rest of his life.

On first appearances the house was quite daunting, with its very high ceilings and celestial stairway that was of such a tremendous scale.

Molly said, "It must lead all the way to heaven."

David said, "Not to be stupid it just went to the upper floors."

Kit and David were very apprehensive at what was going to happen to them.

Molly and Sally were holding hands, giggling and enjoying their new luxurious surroundings. They entered the kitchen; Mrs Baxter had prepared large slices of warm crusty bread, real butter, and ham on the bone alongside a large chocolate cake which immediately sent their taste buds salivating.

Their eyes opened so wide at the sight of the food they looked as if they would pop from their heads at the selection of goodies that were presented in front of them. They sat down as fast as they could, pulling out the old wooden chairs which made a loud scraping noise across the tiles as the children dragged them from under the table in their hurry to seat themselves, Lionel for the moment forgotten. They crammed as much into their mouths as they could, as if they were the disciples seated at the last supper. Mrs Baxter looked on, laughing to herself. These poor mites looked like they had not eaten proper food in months, and when the children rose from the table it was like a swarm of locusts had stripped the surface clean. Now with full tummies, Mrs Baxter took them to their sleeping accommodation. The girls went up the imposing staircase to one of the grander west wing bedrooms that were normally kept free for visiting guests; these were nearer to where Mrs Baxter had her quarters. The boys, to a huge room of enormous proportions over the stables, which Kit thought was nearly as big as his whole house. Looking around the room he perceived there was a small wardrobe and a wooden writing desk which contained pen and paper so they could write to their parents. A leather-bound bible similar to the one that David read in church when attending Sunday school was concealed in one of the drawers. The two beds which were alongside one another were covered with thick grey wool blankets that looked quite cosy and on the wall was a mirror and an old oil painting of horse and hounds hunting. The bathroom was further down the hall next to Preston the chauffeur's quarters.

Climbing into bed that night, they discussed the day's events and what was to happen to them. David dropped off to sleep, but Kit lay awake and heard the whimpering of the two young Labradors that were meant to be sleeping in the tack room. He crept down the stairs, picked up one of the young pups, pulling the other exuberant puppy along by the collar, and took them back up to the bedroom with him. Pushing their fat little bottoms, he helped them on to the bed. Then he snuggled closely to them for comfort. Surrounded by their warmth and the sound of the rise and fall of their breathing with their heads resting over his legs, Kit finally fell asleep. In the early morning the boys returned the dogs to the tack room and the gamekeeper who looked after them was none the wiser.

The boys had both been given a complete new set of clothes consisting of heavy-duty walking boots, a good pair of grey wool trousers and matching tweed jackets. They found when they put them on, they were much too large. Surveying each other in the mirror, they dissolved into hiccupping fits of laughter, unable to stop, each looking more absurd than the other. David said that he looked like an old man and Kit readily agreed.

After a very filling breakfast Mr and Mrs Heart, who owned the estate, said they were free to explore, but not to go near the boating lake or to traumatise any of the animals. Kit and David excitedly ventured outside and made their way along the driveway heading towards the orchard. Mrs Baxter the housekeeper had given them a basket each to fill with apples so Cook could make a pie for tea. David, however, was of an inquisitive nature and climbed over the nearby fence closely followed by Kit who, being of a plumper stature, was finding it difficult to keep up. David surged on ahead, leaving poor Kit lagging behind. It was a complete shock to both of them when they came face to face with the two battling giant stags, antlers entwined, both on their knees locked together in combat. The two boys were completely transfixed. Kit thought how incredibly magnificent and powerful the two animals appeared.

The boys were glued to the spot looking at these beautiful creatures and failed to notice the young stag that had crept silently up behind them. Suddenly Kit felt the hot breath of the challenging animal on his neck followed by its high-pitched rutting whistle. He shouted to David to warn him of the forthcoming danger; the two boys turned, running as fast as they possibly could, both of them too terrified to stop. They were closely followed by the young stag who was making loud clicking noises with his cheek teeth. David, the faster of the two, reached the old oak tree first, clambering up and gaining himself a secure foothold. Kit was puffing and panting behind. David, in his eagerness to pull him to the safety of the lowermost branches, accidentally ripped Kit's sleeve from his new jacket. He was still not fast enough to keep him out of the reach of the rampaging stag's antlers and the animal managed to rip an enormous hole in Kit's new trousers, exposing his pants and his bare bottom to the elements. The two boys remained there for the rest of the afternoon. Too petrified to come down from the tree, they sat hidden amongst the foliage like two monkeys holding onto each other tightly. They were found by the gamekeeper, who, when they failed to return for tea, Cook had sent as a search party too look for them. He couldn't stop smiling to himself when he saw the state of Kit's trousers. He said to the boys, that if it had been a fully-grown stag which had chased them they would not be around to tell the tale. Over the coming months, it was not the only occasion he was to have to come to Kit or David's rescue.

The boys were never brave enough to venture near the stags again. Even when they played the game 'I dare you', which always put them in trouble. Kit, however, always had a reminder of the incident every time he looked at the repair Mrs Baxter had made to his jacket, that is, until he had grown out of it. His trousers, however, never survived, and it was a long time before the bruises faded from his bottom. David, the posher of the two boys, said if he ever met the stag again he'd rather it was on a dinner plate as venison with his knife and fork for protection.

Chapter 21

An unlikely friendship developed between the two boys; under different circumstances they would never have met. David had come from a privileged background, whereas Kit had grown up in a dysfunctional family with a father who was a drunkard and unemployed. Every day to keep them occupied during the time that they were evacuated, the Hearts endeavoured to teach the boys new skills. Their schooling was taken care of in the village where they were enrolled for lessons during the week. At the weekends they would either be under the watchful eye of the gamekeeper or the head stable man who looked after the seven horses that were kept by the Hearts for hunting and riding at leisure. A small young Arab pony was purchased when young David had shown a keen interest in riding. Kit, however, never having had his feet off the ground other than on his swing at home which he had made out of an old tyre, preferred to keep his firmly planted on terra firma. On the days that David would take instruction on riding, Kit would walk the estate with the two Labradors and the gamekeeper, learning how to shoot and skin the rabbits.

David's first riding lesson was taken in the small indoor paddock. The little Arabian colt was brought out already saddled and bridled. The Hearts had purchased him from the local horse fair under the guidance of their stableman. Four white socks, a white blaze down his face, and chestnut in colour, with a long mane and a forelock that covered his eyes, made him very appealing to look at. He stood fourteen hands high without shoes. David, tall for his age, was able to put his foot easily into the stirrup and pull himself up by the pommel into the saddle.

He took to riding like a bird can fly. He had a firm seat and a kind hand and he was often seen cantering over the fields, a small lone figure. Kit was quite envious of David's ability to ride, but being plump, he never had the confidence to try. A strong bond formed between David and the chestnut colt. On a high-pitched whistle he would come to David's call and was easy to catch. He would blow up the pony's nostrils when the colt muzzled him, hoping he'd get an apple or carrot. David would then pull himself astride the colt and sit bareback like a circus rider, trotting him back to the stables to put him into his stall.

It turned out to be a sad loss for David that Sunday evening. The horses had been put away for the night as usual. It had been a beautiful day and the whole household had gone for an afternoon picnic. The Hearts had visitors down from London and under the careful supervision of the staff had gone to the boating lake. The pedal boat that Molly had her accident in was now nowhere to be seen. After playing bowls they swam in the lake, which had seemed warm, gathering its heat from the midday sun hitting the water. They were all exhausted. So, on returning back to the house had retired to bed early. The Hearts and their visitors, having consumed a vast amount of alcohol were now in the land of dreams, making it virtually impossible for them to be woken up. That night nobody heard the four gypsies enter the stable yard. Dressed all in black to conceal themselves, they crept silently through the yard, batons held high in case they encountered any resistance. There was a beam of light coming from the moon which lit the courtyard almost as if an electric light had been switched on, so they had no need for their torches. David and Kit, without the knowledge of the gamekeeper, had taken the dogs to bed with them.

The dogs now useless as they were both snoring loudly on the end of the boys' beds, miserably failing in their duty to alert the family of the intruders.

The four men sneaked stealthily into the stalls, the horses jittery and nervous, tossed their heads with unease. Over their hooves they placed sacks to dull the noise of them clip clopping across the cobbles, and pulled a hood over each horse's head to calm them and prevent them from bolting . They took two apiece including the young Arab, moving as quickly and quietly as they could they led them to the horse boxes which had been carefully hidden in the woods at the end of the drive. The horses went easily into the lorry. Slowly and quietly they drove away into the night, the only observer a young fox cub on a hunting expedition that had paused his late-night activities to watch the lorry disappear before he continued on his way. When the theft was discovered in the morning the police inspector was called. Nobody could understand why the dogs had not barked. David and Kit kept very quiet, realising that they had kept the dogs from doing their duty. The horses were never found. The police said they'd probably been sold to the army, or gone for meat in a different part of the country. This, the boys found very upsetting.

The hearts never purchased any more horses and

had to let the stableman go. They were feeling the pinch now due to the war and decided they could not afford to replace them. David was given the job of looking after the pigs, but he never rode again and was lost without the colt, never having the same affection for the pigs knowing they would be ending up on someone's plate. When the horse fair came to Ascot, David and Kit searched the pens daily in the hope they might find him for sale. The colt, however, was long gone. Regrettably, they never found out where. For quite a few months they scoured the 'for sale' ads in *Horse and Hound*, but eventually gave up looking for him, and sadly for David the colt was never found.

Chapter 22

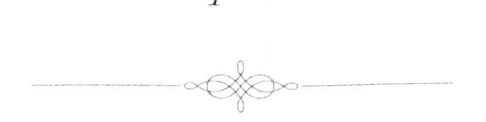

Mrs Baxter sadly died of heart trouble a few months after Sally returned home. Me mum used to say it was cos of all the trouble her and young Molly had caused. Sally stayed good friends with Molly, and when she had her first baby, Sally returned to the estate in Ascot and holidayed again with the Hearts. They were elderly by this time. Molly called her first little baby girl Julia, after Mrs Heart's baby girl that died and was buried in the summer house on the boating lake. The Hearts said they felt humbled by the knowledge that the memory of their daughter Julia would not be forgotten. The girls lost touch with Kit and David. They last heard they'd emigrated to New Zealand. When the two boys returned home to Catford, they found there wasn't much use for the skills they had been taught on the estate. Animal husbandry didn't go down to well on their Curriculum

Vitae when applying for a job in the local bank.

Sid and I, however, had a completely different evacuation story to tell, and how we survived those years to this day, as I still bear the scars I will never know. Life was never to be the same for Sid and I for quite some time.

Sid was a sullen boy. He never spoke to me much when we were at home. He never had any friends, in fact was very much a loner. He was spiteful and cruel to animals and he had no resemblance to me in looks. I often wondered if he was really my brother. In fact, on several occasions, I denied the fact that he was. I used to tell people that Sid was adopted. When me mum found out she gave me a right clip round the ear. I was fed up with always getting Sid's hand-me-downs. They were worn out by the time Sid had outgrown them and the boots always had holes in them. And now more than anything I wished that I had boots that fitted.

Trudging along the track, I wondered where we were going and what was going to happen to us. I wondered where Sally was and if she was going to be alright. I did know one thing, and that was that I did not like this pair of welsh farmers. They seemed to think that Sid and I were going to live with them.

Trying very hard to keep up and not be left behind, I walked along thinking what I should do, I would write to mum, and let her know that a terrible mistake had been made and Dad must come to fetch us and take me and Sidney home immediately. *Yes*, I would write to mum first thing in the morning. Little did I know what a very long wait we were going to have. The muddy track seemed to go on forever, but in the distance, in the fading light, we could see the welcoming glow coming from a rambling old farmhouse building and hear the excited barks from the two shaggy black and white collie dogs that were tied up on a chain outside the barn which stood adjacent to the house. They barked continuously. Sid thought they looked aggressive, I just thought they looked hungry. Our suitcases felt like bags of cement, and all we wanted was a hot tea and something to eat and to go to bed.

Evan and Bronwen, shoved us in the direction of the barn, pushed us both inside and took our suitcases from us. Bronwen's parting words to me and Sid before she swung the big wooden door shut and pulled down the heavy iron bar which secured it tightly locked, were, "I hope your ration books are in these cases, boys. She then turned tail and left to join Evan in the warmth and comfort of the farmhouse.

Outside all we could hear was the continuous whimpering of the two dogs. Wet, hungry, and extremely frightened, I turned to Sid for support. All I got was, "I'm going to punch the daylights out of that bastard in the morning." And then wrapping an old sack round himself which he had found amongst the dirty straw, he promptly rolled over and went to sleep, leaving me sobbing wretchedly and wondering how I could get hold of me mum and dad.

We woke after an unsettled night's sleep, to the creaking sound of the of the bolt being raised. Bronwen entered the barn; in her hands she carried a plate of stale crusty bread. "Breakfast, boys," she said, placing the bread down in front of us. "There's water in the drinking trough outside. And don't dawdle. Sid, you're to go with Evan into the fields. And you, little un, are to help me in the house."

Sid picked up the bread and started to cram it into his mouth. "Looks like this is all we're going to get, Bob. Best eat."

I took one look at the green mould that scaled the outside of the bread, turned my head and started to violently retch into the straw. We could hear Evan's gruff Welsh voice calling us from outside, and went with trepidation into the yard, to see what next misfortune the day was going to unfold. Evan took Sid by the shoulders. Although he was large for his size I looked at him alongside Evan, who had the largest hands I had ever seen and was built like one of the wrestling champions that me dad used to take us to watch sometimes on a Saturday afternoon. Evan whistled the dogs, and I saw Sid disappear into the distance, every so often being given an almighty shove. I knew then that Sid was not about to punch Evan's lights out as he had said last night, and for the time being we were just going to have to do as we were told.

I followed slowly behind Bronwen into the farmhouse. The kitchen was the largest I had ever seen. The floor was covered with large grey slate tiles, that still had a dusting of flour over them where Bronwen had been baking. From the aga which was situated in the heart of the kitchen came the most delicious smells of warm bread just ready to come out of the oven to be eaten. The open wooden shelves which surrounded the kitchen were filled with pots of homemade jams and pickles. My mouth began to water and I looked hopefully at Bronwen. "They're all counted," she said, as her eyes glanced to where my gaze had come to rest. Then handing me a mop and bucket full of soapy water, she said, "Make a good job of that floor, boho or there be no supper for you either."

Sid was faring no better. His boots had started to take in water and he could feel his toes squelching in the mud that was seeping through the small holes that had appeared made from the previous day's walk from the railway station. The dogs kept nipping at his heels, almost as if they knew that he didn't favour them. They arrived at a granite stone wall that had partially fallen down into the field, the large boulders scattered all over as if there had been an earthquake. Evan took a pickaxe out of the bag. "Break up these stones, Sid, and rebuild the wall. I'll be back lunch time." He turned on his heel but not before he gave the dogs the command. "Guard." They immediately dropped to the ground looking intently at Sid, as if he was going to be their next meal.

The kitchen took me all of two hours to clean. I accidentally knocked over the bucket of soapy water, and it felt like I had been cleaning forever. Bronwen had gone into the village to get supplies, and I noticed when she left as well as her purse in her hands she had me and Sid's ration books. The temptation coming from the oven was just too much to bear, I went to the aga and opened the door. Rows and rows of cheese scones met my eyes. They ran in a row of six. I thought if I took one from each row and rearranged them Bronwen would be none the wiser. I ate two as fast as I could, no time to appreciate the melting cheese, or the crumbling comforting feeling of the doughy warm scone as my taste buds savoured the flavour before it hit my grumbling empty tummy. Two in my top pocket and two down my trousers. Just in time before Bronwen returned to inspect the floor. Bronwen entered the kitchen, her shopping bag spilling over with groceries that she had bought with the extra ration vouchers – sugar, flour, and cheese and I was sure I had seen chocolate that Sid and I had very kindly supplied seemingly without our knowledge. "Get those cheese scones out the oven and put them in this basket. They're for delivery for Mrs Thomas up the road, about three mile there and back. It's the little white cottage on the left-hand side with the thatched roof."

I quickly placed the remainder of the uneaten scones into the bag and galloped out the door. It was a very desolate part of Wales we had been evacuated to. All I could see in front of me were fields and fields of sheep.

As I walked through the village I noticed there was just one shop, a small pub, a Methodist church, and few little terraced cottages. The post was handled by the small grocery shop and I had been told that's where we would pick up our mail. If we were lucky enough to receive a letter. I trudged on, thinking perhaps I should run away, but I had no idea where we were I could have been in a foreign country because I couldn't even understand the sing-song dialect that was spoken by the locals that I encountered on my way to deliver the scones to Mrs Thomas.

I knocked on the door; it was opened by a jolly-looking woman. In fact, she had appeared pleasant until she opened the bag and counted the scones. "They're six short," she said. With that she took back the brown envelope that I had given her and before returning it to me, wrote on the back, 'six short', took out a few brass pennies, and closed the door abruptly. It took me over an hour to walk back to the farm. Now starting to rain, I was soaked through to the skin. Evan and the two collie dogs joined me at the fork in the road that led back up to the farm. Sid's shoulders were hunched. He was caked in dirt, and his hands were bleeding and covered in blisters. He didn't talk, just grunted an acknowledgement of recognition and as we walked back to the farm together, the two collies closely behind, every so often biting our heels, herding us onwards as if we were sheep.

Bronwen opened the door, hand outstretched, waiting for the envelope. She read what was written on the back and knew immediately I had taken the scones, and on counting the pennies that she had been short changed. "No supper for you, boys. We have a thief, Evan. We've taken in a thief." Bronwen marched me and Sid back to the barn, our palatial living quarters, locking us in for the night. Sid looked like he was going to strike me dead. I reached down inside my trousers and took out two of the remaining now pungent-smelling scones. Sid's face broke into a grin. He grabbed them from me and ate them, cramming as much of them into his mouth as he possibly could. The cheese now hard and the scones now stale, but I don't think anything tasted so good to him. We then settled down for another cold and miserable night. Later on, when Sid was snoring I heard the two collies whimpering outside. Stretching my hand as far as I could under the gap in the barn door, I passed the two remaining cheese scones out. The two hungry dogs devoured them ravenously. A small black nose appeared under the door and a long pink tongue brushed across my hand in thanks, and I knew I had made a friend.

The night seemed interminably long, I could smell Sid from where I lay across from him in the straw. It reminded me of Mum cooking cabbage without the window open, or the smell of bad fish that you got sometimes when you walked through the docks on a sunny day. Neither of us had washed for two days, or changed our clothes. We were tired, hungry, and very homesick for Mum and Dad. In the corner of the barn throughout the night I could hear scurrying noises, and the straw would move as if by magic and you would hear strange squeals and squeaks. Sid had gone straight to sleep, but I lay awake wondering, where Sally was, and how I could let Mum and Dad know what was happening and where we were.

In the morning, we could hear the wind and rain battering against the door. It sounded like a real storm. We had no idea of the time and it was still dark. Evan threw open the barn door. "Get yourself together, boys, we're to bring the sheep down from the hills, to the lower pastures. We're in for some bad weather." Bronwen had wrapped a bread and jam sandwich for each of us in some brown paper. We followed Evan out of the barn, eating as we went, knowing that was all we were going to get for the rest of the day. The two dogs were tight to Evan's heel, although every now and again they would run to me and wag their tails as if we had some private secret, only to be brought to check swiftly by Evan with his shepherd's stick and shrill short whistle. We trudged through the farmyard, passing Gobbler the turkey. Sid had called him that because of the strange noise he made; he had attacked us a few times already but he let us pass unheeded, keeping a wary eye on the two dogs. He was a large bird with a wrinkly red chin that hung down to his breast, and enormous wings that flapped aggressively at you. Sid and I had never seen the like of such a bird, not even at the zoo, because by the time one of his relatives reached our table at Christmas, he would bear no resemblance to this fighting, flying creature that stood in front of us, on this occasion letting us go through the yard with no trouble.

The walk to the upper pasture was long and steep. Our coats, which were totally unsuitable for the occasion, were soaked. The wind grew wilder the higher we went and Sid, although strong and tall, was bent double. I hung on tightly to the back of his jacket in the fear I would roll back down the steep hill and disappear never to be seen again. Evan, however, strode ahead treating the storm like it was a scenic walk in the park. Living in Wales all his life, he was used to the frequent torrential downpours, and the violent snow storms that covered the hills, leaving the animals vulnerable and often impossible to find if they had fallen into a deep snow drift. A fine sleet filtered through the early morning mist and it was damp underfoot.

By the time we reached the sheep they looked like bundles of cotton wool piled in a heap. Their backs were against the wall trying to shield themselves from the weather as they were first-time mothers, nervous and fidgety, edging closely to one another for comfort. A small flock of sixty, most of them were in lamb. Frightened and vulnerable, huddled together in the corner of the field, Sid and I watched in awe as the two dogs, Meg and Piper, responded immediately to the sharp whistle instructions coming from Evan. He turned the sheep towards us and with the aid of the two dogs waved his arms in an attempt to keep the frightened animals together.

We walked them as quickly as we could to the lower fields where they could lamb safely. We reached the paddock and the dogs herded the sheep forward. Sid opened the gate to let them pass inside. It swung loosely on its hinges and it took all of Sid's strength to hold it open and stop it dropping into the deep mud which would make it impossible to close. The sheep in their eagerness to escape, the dogs rushed forward, trying to pass through the narrow gap six or seven at a time, making loud bleating sounds as if in awful pain. They had no thought for anyone that was in their path. Sid, in his ignorance, failed to move out the way in time. I saw him fall to the ground and disappear under their hoofs. The ewes, who were on a desperate mission to reach the safety of the field, had pushed Sid to the ground. At that moment in time I realised I still loved my brother.

Thinking I had lost him for good, petrified, I ran forward to try and stop the surge of animals as one by one they trampled over Sid. Evan pulled me back and for a brief moment I thought I saw compassion in his eyes. When the last ewe entered the field, I ran to where Sid lay. His eyes were closed and his face was covered in dirt. His nose seemed to have shifted to the other side of his face. "Sid," I said. "You can't die on me." As I took him by the shoulders, as heavy as he was, to try and hold him to me, his eyes opened and he sat up.

"Jesus," he said. "I won't be doing that again in a hurry."

With that he got slowly and awkwardly to his feet. Evan clipped him round the ear for taking the Lord's name in vain, and we walked back to the farm, Sid limping clumsily behind. Sid's nose remained crooked for the rest of his life and he always told the girls he got it in the boxing ring. That moment of brotherly love, I never felt again. Sid was always careful after that to get out of the way of any stampeding animals and he continued to be his disagreeable self for the remainder of our time in Wales. His crooked nose remained his most prominent feature all his life.

Chapter 23

Life settled into a routine. We would be up every morning at four. I used to wonder what the sun looked like. It never seemed to shine in Wales. Breakfast would be a bit of old stale bread; if we were very lucky and Bronwen was feeling generous she might put jam on it, but that was not very often. Sid hated the animals, he had no sympathy for them when Evan would slaughter one of them. He would always laugh at me when I cried, remembering how I had helped them come into the world. I tried never to get too friendly with any of the lambs, knowing that they were destined for someone's dinner. Although it certainly was not Sid's or mine. Evan would come to the barn at any time during the night and haul one of us out to help with a ewe that was in difficulty lambing. We would hold the torch high in the air, frozen to the bone, and watch Evan as he pulled and tugged a dead lamb deep from the womb, sometimes laying its lifeless body outstretched in the snow. More than once a ewe would give birth to twins and Evan would skin the dead lamb and tie it to one of the healthy twins, in an attempt to disguise the lamb and give it to a mother who'd lost hers. This did not always work and so sometimes we would end up bottle feeding them in the barn.

The weather that winter was turbulent and the snow storms became more violent and the drifts deeper. It became dangerous to wander too far from the farm. Evan would take the tractor along what used to be the muddy track and try and clear it, Sid walking ahead trying to shovel the snow into piles at the side of the road. If we were lucky and the weather eased, Bronwen would send either Sid or me into the village to pick up the rations. This could sometimes take all day because of the long queues we would encounter at the village shop. I would always ask if there were any letters for Sid or me, but there never was, and I felt that me mum had abandoned us.

This particular day it had stopped snowing, and Bronwen had sent me into the village to get some fresh supplies and deliver some of her scones. After the first incident of short changing Mrs Thomas on her delivery, I never did it again. Evan had taken his belt to me that day, and I still had the scars on me back to show. It was a long walk into the village, and I had been told many times not to wander off the main track. That day, for reasons unknown to myself I decided to climb the gate at the end of the road that led into the village, and take what I thought was a short cut through the woods and the neighbouring farmland, taking at least a mile and a half off my journey. Sid was mucking out the barn, and Evan had gone shooting for rabbit with the dogs.

The further I got into the woods the more concerned I became. The weather had begun to change; the sun had disappeared and the sky had become ominously dark through the overhead trees. I was relieved when the woods started to thin out and revealed the open field as in the distance I could now see the tops of the village houses of Garndiffaith. Starting to run before the weather got any worse, my eyes looking directly ahead, unaware of the danger underneath my feet, they suddenly disappeared from under me, I fell for what seemed minutes. I had stumbled across the entrance to a disused mine shaft that had had been concealed by a large mound of snow. I must have plummeted at least fifteen feet and on reaching the bottom of the shaft hit my head hard on the ground. Luckily the bag of scones had fallen with me and lay scattered on the floor. These, I was very grateful for over the next few days as I feared I could have died from lack of nourishment. Thankfully, my fall had been broken by a mound of old sacks and I was relatively unhurt. But I saw no way out of my predicament and was convinced that this was going to be the end of me.

When I failed to return that night Evan and Bronwen presumed that I had run away. Sid said that I didn't have the guts for it, and they had better look for me, as Mum and Dad would come and sort them out if anything had happened. The next morning Evan organised a search party – a few of the local villagers volunteered. They took the dogs and went out scouring the countryside, but I had wandered quite a long way off the main track. When it started to get dark they returned home to their suppers, being unsuccessful in their endeavour to find me. I sat that night wrapped in sacks and eating the remains of the cheese scones, with only the occasional inquisitive mouse for company. Sid was not about to give up. I was still his brother. Early the next day, he rose from his bed. Bronwen, as the weather had got colder and the barn had filled with orphaned lambs, had allocated Sid and me a room in the house. It had an old wooden bed with half the slats missing so you would often fall right through to the floor, but it was warmer, if not more comfortable than the straw. There was a white porcelain wash basin in the corner, that every so often, if you were lucky, would release a spurt of cold running water, enabling us to wash some of the smells of the farm away.

Sid, so as not to awake Evan, crept with boots in his hand and descended down the creaking narrow staircase that led directly into the kitchen. He went out into the yard and released Meg and Piper from their kennel, placed one of my smelly old socks in front of Meg's nose and gave her the direction to go forward and seek. This command Sid had heard Evan give her many times before when hunting rabbits. The two dogs ran ahead, eager to please, noses to the ground. Luckily it had not snowed over the last few days, and when Sid came to the end of the track he could still see the imprint of my shoes where I had climbed over the fence. Sid laboured through the snow, the dogs leaping and jumping in front of him in eager anticipation, barking loudly, Sid calling my name over and over again.

I heard the dogs first, then Sid, and shouted as loud as I could. Meg and Piper reached the shaft first, digging away at the mound of snow. Sid peered over the edge of the gaping chasm, looking down, and said,

"Well Bob, you're in a bit of a hole. I better get help so we can get you out of there." He returned an hour later, with rope, some lads from the village and a wooden bucket. They lowered it down, and climbing in with one foot and clinging on as tightly as I possibly could to the rope, Sid brought me back into the daylight, the dogs excitedly jumping up at me with the pleasure of being reunited with a lost friend. Leaning on Sid's shoulder, we walked together, for once as brothers united, back to the farm through the snow.

I was none the worse for my adventure, but both Sid and I got a severe beating. Me for eating the scones and Sid for taking the dogs into the fields without Evan's permission.

Winter turned to spring and the snow started to disappear. The colour of the landscape changed from brilliant white, to a mixture of emerald green and yellow. The sun started to shine and the lambs could be seen in the fields leaping over each other and jumping like the Jack in the box toy we'd had as small boys. Their little tails could be seen wiggling in every direction, and I thought it extremely cruel that Evan would tie a large rubber band round them and we would find them lying in the fields where they had dropped off. Sometimes in the summer months the ewes would get sheep blown, where the flies laid their eggs deep into their skin, causing extreme distress to the ewe. Evan and Sid would then cut the offending maggots out with a knife. I could never do this however hard I tried.

There was an abundance of lamb everywhere, and Sid and I often would smell the succulent meat roasting in the oven alongside the richly browned vegetables, but the whole time we were there we never were allowed to taste it. We lived on bread and jam and if we were lucky sometimes we had a hot cup of tea. Sometimes Sid and I would steal the eggs from under the disgruntled hens before Bronwen had time to collect them and we would pierce them and eat them raw. Many a hen went as Sunday dinner because Bronwen thought they were a bad layer. Evan and Bronwen, to keep up appearances would take us to the Methodist church to make the locals think that they were God-fearing people. We would have to put on our spare pair of trousers. I was always frightened they would wear out, so never sat down in them properly but just perched on the edge of the pew, thinking that I would never get another pair. We would be made to nod and smile at the neighbours, Evan's strong grip holding onto us as he would march us away, daring us to voice our unhappiness, whispering under his breath threats of more thrashings if we revealed our circumstances to any of the congregation.

I started to get sick. The lack of good food was beginning to show on my young body. I'd broken out in sores and had started to cough and developed asthma. Sid looked like a hardened criminal, and we still hadn't heard from Mum and Dad. Life was unbearably hard. The other children we came across who had been evacuated to the village hardly spoke. Always too busy with their duties. There was one boy called Tom, who I sometimes met up with when we were on our delivery errands. He was a tall boy with very long legs and arms, which protruded from his clothes. He had exceptionally large ears and he always reminded me of a large stick insect that I'd once seen in a book. He lived with an old farming couple who as long as he got his work done left him very much alone. He was always glad when we met up as I believed him to be quite lonely as nobody spoke to him very much. He lived not far from us in Camberwell. We always promised to meet up when we got sent back home. But we never did. Years later, I read in the paper he had robbed and murdered a local woman. I often wondered what had driven him to that action.

But I remembered one incident that I had conveniently chosen to forget, thinking perhaps it had always been inside him waiting to come out.

Tom and I had been walking to the village together. We were on our way to pick up the rations. We had been walking for about a mile when we passed David Jones's cottage. We could see that he had fallen over in his front garden and the cottage door was wide open. He was hardly breathing and had clawed at the snow in his attempt to get back to the cottage. I knew that we should run and get help. But before I could go to Mr Jones' aid, Tom took me by the shoulders, giving me a shake. "This is too good an opportunity to miss," he said, going inside the cottage. I followed closely behind.

I watched as he went through drawer after drawer, opening and shutting them as if he were a trained burglar and had done it all before, leaving no evidence that he had even looked inside. He shoved into his pockets anything he found of value, including a little gold locket that had belonged to Mr Jones' dead wife. Looking back, I am ashamed to say I did nothing to stop him. When we went back outside I think Mr Jones was already dead. Tom gave him a vicious kick. "That's for all you Welsh bastards," he said under his breath. Then looking at me, told me that this would be our secret. He ran off. I avoided him after that, thinking him to be a very unpleasant boy because of what he'd done. I always felt guilty about Mr Jones, wondering if I'd helped him would he have lived? But this, I shall never know.

We often wondered why me mum never wrote. Bronwen told us she thought Mum and Dad had died in one of the bombing raids. Or, that they no longer wanted us.

Sid never seemed to take much notice of Bronwen's stories, it was only me that took them to heart and cried myself to sleep nearly every night. He used to call her a spiteful old cow. He knew it wouldn't be long and we'd be going home, that's what he tried to make himself believe, although I think even Sid had his doubts about Mum and Dad coming for us. And in the end, it was him who saved the day.

Chapter 24

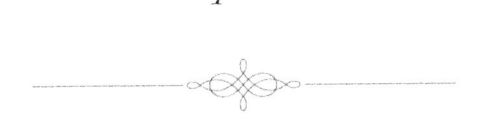

Sid had been very spiteful towards me. Over the last few days. I had been feeling very miserable.

It was a Tuesday morning. I remember it well because it was the day Sid went AWOL. Sid had gone up to the Easter pasture. We called it that because that's where the young ewes were kept just before they lambed, which always seemed to be around Easter. As he walked across the field and climbed over the gate he heard the desperate bleating before he saw what the cause of the disturbance was. The ewes were running around in all directions – they looked terrified. They were being chased by one of the village dogs which was out of control and barking incessantly. One of the ewes had got her head firmly stuck between the bars of the gate. Her eyes were rolling and she was thrashing and pulling from left to right in an attempt to free herself. Sid thought she was going to die, so he opened the gate to try and release her and to calm her down. For a brief moment he took his eyes away from the other ewes who were running and jumping completely out of control as they were chased round and round the field by a large brown unidentifiable mongrel who was nipping aggressively at their heels. Before he could stop them half a dozen of the sheep had run past him and down the lane. He sent Meg back into the field to chase off the marauding stray dog, but not before he saw the runaways disappearing into the distance. They were heading towards Mrs Thomas', which was two miles further on. It took him twenty minutes to restore order and release the distressed ewe's head from the five-bar gate. The ewe, now seeming none the worse for her ordeal, had joined the others, who had gone back to chewing the cud. Meg had now successfully chased off the unwelcome canine that had pursued the sheep causing so much chaos. So Sid then whistled Meg, sending her forward to try and find the escaping fugitives.

They had not run very far. He found them a little further on; they had entered Mrs Thomas' garden, who always left her front gate ajar because the catch was broken. The first three had dropped to the grass, already squirming in agony, kicking their stomachs with their hoofs in the hope to find some relief. One dead already, the others on their knees as if they were about to be slaughtered. Mrs Thomas stood at the door with a smirk on her face. "They've eaten the poison yew in the garden, they're all going to die."

Sid looked in horror at the scene that was taking place in front of his eyes and knew that there was to be no reprieve for these dying animals. He could not help them. Sid knew he would be in for another severe beating. The deaths of the six ewes would be a large financial loss to Evan and he would be uncontrollable in his anger and in dishing out his punishment, in that split second, he knew he couldn't go back to the farm. He turned to Mrs Thomas and said, "Tell young Bob I'll be back for him."

So, without a brass farthing in his pocket, he turned around and walked slowly up the road and away from the dying sheep and Mrs Thomas's front garden. His only intention now to go home and find Mum and Dad.

Sid was going home. He didn't know how he would get there or even if he would still find his mum and dad, but he knew that neither Bob nor himself could endure any more physical and mental abuse from Evan and Bronwen. He headed through the village, pulling his collar up around him. He took no comfort from the threadbare material that had now worn into holes and had seen better days. Walking towards the main road, not sure whether to head for the railway station or the busy carriageway, which the large delivery lorries travelled up and down taking supplies all over the country. Having no money in his pocket, decided for him. He took the right fork away from the station and headed towards the busy road.

Sid walked for what seemed to be hours and hours. The sun had started to go down and was disappearing slowly in front of his eyes. Darkness was creeping in around him. He felt the tiredness seep through his body and finally gave in, sinking to the ground underneath an overgrown hedgerow. He laid out his jacket on the floor in attempt to make himself comfortable, then fell into a disturbed sleep due to his strange surroundings and worrying what would become of young Bob. Sid dreamt of home.

Evan was so angry that Sid had left; he'd lost a great deal of money from the death of the ewes and with no one else to vent his anger on, he took his belt to me again and again. It was only Bronwen who finally pulled Evan away, before he did irreversible damage, that finally made him stop. I do believe he got sadistic pleasure out of the beatings. His eyes would light up and he would build the beating up into a wild crescendo, until finally smiling, completely exhausted, he would then sit back in his old leather armchair in the kitchen. He would then request a cup of tea from Bronwen, then, yawning, tell her how tiring it was, disciplining us boys into obedience.

Chapter 25

It was an early start for Sid; the dawn chorus and the dew dripping from the hedgerow onto his face startled him. For a moment he was unaware of where he was. Then, looking around and realising how wet his clothes were, he remembered yesterday's events. Gathering up his damp coat and folding it over his arm, he now had the appearance of an old tramp. Sid had no idea where he was going, or how far he would have to travel, or how long it would take, but now he strode deliberately on with the intent of reaching the busy road which was not far in front of him. He could already hear the roaring of the heavy traffic speeding along the highway. Immediately increasing his pace, he turned the corner, and when the lane opened up onto the main road he cautiously stepped out, keeping well to the side of the road and with the confidence of an experienced hitch hiker stuck out his thumb, trying to avoid the continuous flow of traffic. It was at least an hour before he was offered a lift. Sid was unkempt and had the appearance of an undesirable, with his twisted nose, crooked grin, and dirty clothes. But finally, a lorry pulled up beside him and the driver leant over and opened the cab door.

"Where you going, sonny?"

"Blackheath, sir, if you know it," Sid replied eagerly.

"I'm going straight into London to the meat market, Smithfield. I can drop you there. I've got a load of fresh carcass to unload."

Reaching over, he pulled Sid safely up into the cab and introduced himself as Sammy, revved the engine, and away they went, Sid leaving his brother and Garndiffaith far behind.

Sammy was jovial and put Sid at ease very quickly. He passed Sid over a bacon sandwich as they talked; he was intrigued by the boy and his unfortunate appearance. Sid nearly choked in his eagerness to consume the chunky white crusty bread and the thick fatty bacon that fell out of the side, there was so much of it, gulping it down as if he hadn't eaten in weeks. The heat from the radiator warmed him through and Sid began to relax. Sammy started to question him about the state of his appearance, and how he came to be hitchhiking. Sid began his story.

Sammy listened intently over the next three hours in complete shock from Sid's revelations. He couldn't believe two kids could have been treated so badly. When they drove into Smithfield Market four hours later, Sid was sound asleep, completely exhausted from talking, not even waking up when Sammy unloaded the meat. Sammy cleaned up, washed the lorry down then drove Sid back to his younger sister who lived in Camberwell. They gave him a hot meal, a hot bath, and a bar of chocolate and put him to bed. Luckily there was no evacuation into the shelter that night and Sid slept soundly. The faraway sounds of the bombs and the sirens failed to wake or alert him of forthcoming dangers. It had been a long time since Sid had slept on a real mattress and Sammy and his sister Brenda, when they looked in on him, heard the heavy breathing of a young man in a deep contented sleep that even the sound of a volcanic eruption could not have woken.

It was eight o'clock in the morning by the time Sid climbed sleepily from his bed. Sammy had looked him out a jumper and a pair of his trousers. The jumper was a little too big and the trousers too short but they were clean and hole-free. Brenda had cooked him a thick slice of bacon with egg, toast, sausage, and beans. She used most of their remaining coupons, but it was worth it to see Sid eating with such enjoyment. To Sid this was a feast and he ate with gusto, pushing as much into his mouth as he could as if it were going to be his last meal for some time. While Sid slept Sammy had been making enquiries with the war office. He knew a girl there who was sweet on him, and with a joint effort they had managed to locate a telephone number for Bert.

Sammy called Bert and explained the situation. Within the hour, Bert was banging on the door, Connie standing closely behind, eagerly waiting to see Sid. When the door opened she ran to Sid, sobbing, "My boy. My boy." She could not believe how Sid had grown. Standing in front of her was a young man. No longer a boy. He had left his childhood behind in Garndiffaith. He looked at Mum, but there was no warm embrace.

Sally said later, "He had a coldness about him." He wore this like a coat for the rest of his life.

Sid just stood there. "Why didn't you come for us, Dad?"

"We wrote."

His hands staying rigidly by his side, he was unable

to return Mum's embrace. It turned out Mum never got our letters. Why, I don't know. Perhaps Bronwen never sent them. Evan and Bronwen had written regularly to me mum saying what good boys we were and how well we were doing at school. She had even forged a footnote on the bottom of the letter as if it had come from us boys telling Mum how much we were enjoying ourselves and not to bother to make the tedious journey to come and see us because it was too dangerous to travel. Mum, thinking we were safe and being well fed, thought we were better off and didn't want to unsettle us with a visit. Dad was so angry when he heard this. Sid had never seen him so angry. He went immediately and fetched Uncle Jimmy. Nobody was going to treat his boys this way and get away with it. Mum would have liked to have met Bronwen and given her a good ticking off, but Dad said he didn't want to be looking out for her too. Sammy, who remembered Dad from school days, went with them as well. "Safety in numbers and all that," he said. So they all got into Dad's Morris Ten and drove down to Wales to fetch me home.

Chapter 26

I had no notion when I got up that morning, that it was to be my last day in Garndiffaith. My back hurt from the terrible beating I had received, and Sid, I thought was gone for good. I wasn't sure if he had been murdered by Evan in a moment of spontaneous anger, when discovering the death of the sheep. Mrs Thomas had asked them to be removed from her front garden without delay. Evan and I had taken the truck and loaded them on. They were not suitable for human consumption due to the nature of their unfortunate death. So we were going to burn the carcasses later on in the day. I felt sad looking at them. I wondered if Mrs Thomas had poisoned Sid , as he had disappeared completely and I had not seen him since breakfast the previous day.

I made my way down the stairs and out into the yard; Gobbler flew at me in his usual belligerent manner, knocking me to the ground, covering me in mud, making me look just like I was about to go on an army combat mission. The blood had started to seep through the back of my shirt and my arms hurt from the bruises where Evan had held me down. The stench from the pile of rotting sheep that Evan had not burnt yet hit my nostrils. As I passed them, taking in their blank vacant staring eyes, I thought that perhaps they were better off. I walked on, wondering what "Another day in Paradise" would reveal. Sid and I did not get on, but he had been my only companion and being the eldest, I had always looked to him for protection.

I picked myself up from the mud and flapped my arms frantically at Gobbler on my way into the barn to get on with the first chore of the morning, collecting the eggs for Evan and Bronwen's breakfast. Then, feed the dogs and clean the yard. Then back into the fields to repair the stone walls that were constantly falling down. It was way past lunchtime, when I saw the little grey Morris Ten winding up the road in the distance, making its way at what would be considered a very dangerous speed up the narrow lane. It pulled into the yard, scattering Gobbler and the chickens in every direction. Three men got out of the car and stood in the yard. From a distance it was hard to see, but my heart missed a beat, and a sudden overwhelming feeling of relief came upon me. I was sure without a doubt that I was looking at Jimmy and me dad. Who the other chap was, I had no idea. I threw the pickaxe to the ground and ran as fast as my legs would let me without falling over back down to the farm, waving my arms frantically in case they got back into the car and disappeared without having seen me. "Dad, I'm here. I'm here!" I shouted.

Dad turned round. In front of him stood a boy he hardly recognised – undernourished, face covered in sores, and wearing clothes that were much too big, making me look like I had been put in the wash and shrunk. He walked slowly forward. "I've come to take you home, Bob. You're coming home." He picked me up. I weighed as little as a bag of flour, and he gently put me in the back of the car. "We're going to fetch your things, Bob," he said.

"Ain't got no things anymore, Dad," I said.

The three of them went striding up to the front door and hammered violently on it with their fists. Evan opened the door.

"You Evan?" Dad said it like he'd come from a cowboy movie. Evan nodded, and before he could put his hands up to protect himself, me dad raised his fist high and with one knockout punch and a hefty kick each from Jimmy and Sammy, left him lying ungracefully sprawled on the doorstep. Dad turned round looked back over his shoulder as he left and said, "That was for my boys."

The three of them then got back into the car, Dad wrapped a blanket round me legs, and we all drove back to Blackheath to find Mum. Walking into the house, it felt like it was all a dream. Sally and me Mum and Sid were all stood waiting. Mum had baked a treacle pudding just for me. Nothing looked the same. Sally was all grown up and spoke very posh and was wearing a dress that made her look far too old for her age. Mum was fat. She looked old, and it looked like somebody had drawn lines on her face with a pencil. Sid was all cleaned up and in the short time that he had been home, with clean clothes and food inside him, looked almost handsome.

Mum looked at the scars that could be seen on my arms and started to cry. "Oh Bob, what have they done to you?" Then marched me upstairs for a hot bath, and to rub cream into the open sores that covered my face and body. We never heard what happened to Evan. Dad told the authorities about what they'd done to Sid and me, but because of the war, they slipped through the net as far as punishment was concerned, but I don't think they took on any more evacuees.

Chapter 27

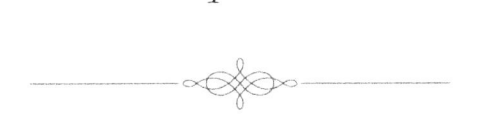

Pressing my nose flat against the window, I blew onto the glass. The condensation slowly started to clear, giving me an unclouded view over the top of the Greenwich skyline. Through the window, I could now see the catastrophic damage that had been done to the terraced house opposite. It had been completely destroyed, almost like an earthquake had miraculously swallowed it up in the night. There was just a very large crater where the house had been, filled now with number 24's entire life. Suitcases and clothes, old pictures, and a rusty old pram were being wheeled away from the debris by a little boy aged about seven, who was filling it as fast as he could with anything of value.

"They all got out," me mum said, as she entered the attic with two steaming mugs of tea. "That is except Arthur the cat. I don't think we'll see him again in a hurry."

Things just returned to normal, if you knew what normal was. We were still at war, Jimmy still ran the local black market, and Dad still tried to keep the car lot going. Why, I don't know. There was hardly any business. Sid joined Jimmy in his escapades and the two of them were always ducking and diving, trying keep out of trouble from the law. Phyllis had joined the war office and had taken a secretarial course. Dad was very proud of her, but he didn't let on much in front of me mum, cos she still got upset and had never really forgiven Phyllis. The bombs still rained down on London and many a night we spent in the air raid shelter in the back yard, the four of us. Sid, me, Mum and Sally, with just a hot flask, a bunch of sandwiches and a torch. We'd play games, like scrabble and charades, but Sid always won because he cheated, and if you questioned his honesty he could become quite disagreeable. It was always a great relief when we heard the all-clear siren and our house was still upright.

When we emerged from the darkness, Mum would tell us how lucky we had been. Sid and I couldn't always see the lucky side of things.

It was cold and smelly, and it was always a great

relief when we emerged into the daylight. And we were all in one piece. Though after hours of being imprisoned with Sid, I often wondered how we had all survived at all. We would return to our daily duties, Mum always saying a little thank you prayer to the picture of Jesus that was on the wall in the front parlour. So very grateful that the house hadn't disappeared into oblivion like number 24 opposite.

In the school holidays, I would help Dad clean the cars in the lot. I'd make them shine until you saw your face in them for which I earned a few pennies for my trouble. Dad's car was a Morris Ten. It was his pride and joy. He'd rescued it from a house that had been badly bombed. The car had been in the garage and Dad had been asked to take the car away for scrap by the owner who had no use for it. Instead, Jimmy and Dad had pieced the car together bit by bit, turning it from an old rust bucket into the gleaming automobile that it was. Dad had given me the job that day of cleaning it inside and out and it gleamed in the bright sunlight like a brand-new car just off the production line. Before I had put the last finishing touches to what I proudly thought was a work of art, it had started to rain. Not wanting my handiwork to be spoilt, I thought I would put the car away in the outbuilding that stood on the car lot. It was at the bottom of a small slope and the door to it was already wide open. Not being able to drive, I thought I could open the car door, take off the handbrake and steer it into the shed.

I released the handbrake, not realising the car was so heavy. It gathered momentum. The steering locked and it was impossible to manoeuvre it in the right direction. The car gathered speed down the slope with me hanging onto the steering wheel for grim death. I tried with all my strength to dig my heels into the tarmac and secure a footing to try and head the car in the direction of the open door. It careered off course and missed the open door by at least a foot, hitting the wall with a loud bang. I realised instantly I had made a big mistake. The front of the car folded like a concertina. The glass from the shattered headlights lay on the floor like thousands of tiny hailstones, or a biscuit that had broken into crumbs when it had fallen from the packet. Looking at the damage, I realised how angry Dad would be. I left the car where it stood, wrote an apology letter to Dad, and cycled home as fast as I could in the hope that Dad would cool down before I'd have to see him again, and would have to listen to his ranting and ravings at how stupid I was.

He did eventually forgive me, but not for quite

some time. I was always very careful after that. Eventually Dad taught me to drive and Mum said that she was surprised we still managed to stay friends, although he never ceased to remind me of the incident, right up until he died.

Chapter 28

We were growing up; the war ended in 1945. Sally was now a beautiful young woman, Sid had developed an interest in girls, and I was just interested in cars. Hitler had committed suicide and VE day was celebrated on the 8th May of that year. Our street was closed off, everybody threw a party.

There were fireworks, balloons, banners, and we danced all night. The royal family appeared with Winston Churchill on the balcony at Buckingham Palace. Celebrations went on right into the night. Everybody was so intensely happy. We had been liberated. We could all now look forward to the future. I started working for me dad and Sid. Well, Sid did his own thing. What, we were never quite sure. Mum said as long as he brought no trouble home and the housekeeping was paid, she left him alone. That was until he started drinking.

Every morning me mum would get up and make us all a cooked breakfast before we left the house. I would ride on my bicycle to Bert's Empire, as me dad called it. Sid would disappear, sometimes not returning till the early hours of the morning. Sally went to college. She was the clever one. I was good with cars and a quick learner, but the car lot wasn't that busy, and me wages were poor. Sid, however, always had a pocket full of notes. Where they came from, no one liked to ask, cos if they did, they would always be told to mind their own business. I was jealous of Sid, the smart clothes, the girls he bragged about, and when he came home with a brand-new motorbike, I'd had enough. He never was that generous with me mum and she always had to demand the household money from him. Because as much as Sid had, he never gave it willingly. I spoke to me dad about having a raise in me wages but me dad said, "I just can't afford it, lad. We'll have to find you something else."

Big Joe was one of Dad's customers and was a good friend to Dad over the years. He'd lent Dad money during the war when things had gotten really tough, and as he had no children of his own he looked on Dad as his son. I was fed up with having no money. Sid always seemed to flash the cash. He never gave any to Mum though, and she was always short. She would always make sure that Sid was alright. To this day, I'll never know why he stole from her. He treated her with such contempt and always laughed at her behind her back. He was always coming home late, or drunk. It was funny though, he never brought home any girls. Sally always said, once they'd found out how disagreeable he was, they never wanted to see him again.

Sid didn't seem to have love for anyone, or anything. Uncle Jimmy said, "When he was born they forget to give him a heart." To this day, I often wonder if he was right.

Sally learnt to avoid Sid, especially when he had too much to drink. That way if we didn't speak to him everything ran along smoothly. It was only if Sid was short of money there were arguments. Especially when he would steal from me mum or take my wage packet.

Joe was a lighterman on the barges working for E. W. Taylor situated in Dunbar wharf, Limehouse. To become a lighterman you had to become an apprentice and serve under a master. The privilege of becoming an apprentice passed from father to son. Big Joe had worked on the River Thames all his life as his father had before him. It could be a dangerous job and you had to have a good knowledge of the tides and be sure footed. The barges would sway from side to side and in the winter when walking round the gunnel you had to be very careful not to fall into the murky fast-flowing tidal waters and drown. Dad asked Big Joe if he could get me a job. It was good money on the barges, and Joe somehow managed to slide me in the back door. It was an early start, but I was keen and willing to learn. A few of the lighterman were angry that I'd got the apprenticeship. I wasn't a blood relative to Joe and it should have been handed down father to son. They would always give me the really difficult job of rowing the barge and I built up large muscles in my upper arms. I didn't mind it, always used to impress the girls.

Life was good, the apprenticeship was six years. After two years I was able to apply to be a Freeman. I sailed through all the exams and Dad was very proud. I worked with a young chap called Tricky Dickie. He was a bit of a wide boy and he had been given his apprenticeship by his dad. He wasn't much of a worker and was always looking to make a quick buck. Every morning we would be given our instructions telling us which wharf to go to. We'd collect the barge to take up the river which had been loaded for delivery by the dockers. It was a four thirty in the morning start and it was always cold and foggy, but I loved it. I was nimble and sure footed, learnt from my boxing days, and I earned a bit of a reputation for the speed I could get round the gunnel without slipping. Dickie was lazy and a bit clumsy, and as we never wore safety lines I was always grabbing hold of his jacket to stop him disappearing over the side.

Dickie had got himself into a bit of bother; he gambled and drank excessively and owed quite a bit of money to some real unsavoury characters who had been hanging around the docks. Without my knowledge, he'd arranged to offload some of the cargo out the back door to pay off his debt, but he did this once too often. Customs already had their eyes on Dickie for other things, so when they had been tipped off by personage unknown they had been quick to act on the information that Dickie was stealing. Early one morning they banged on the door and searched both our houses top to bottom.

Mum was demented. Dickie had given me mum a bottle of scotch for her birthday from his spoils and they took that away for evidence. They marched me away, thinking I was in on it. I was asked to leave E. W. Taylor, although nothing was ever proved, even though Dickie tried to pin it all on me. Mum was right upset and Dad didn't talk to me for some time.

Dickie, however, got away with it but a year later I heard that he fell over the side blind drunk and drowned. Me mum said he'd got his comeuppance.

Chapter 29

I went back to work with me dad when I came off the water. They gave me a bit of severance pay which cushioned the blow of having to leave, which I put aside. Dad wasn't too pleased with me. Phyllis was unwell at the time and he wanted to spend more time with her. Things started to pick up in the motor trade and me and Dad were doing quite well. Uncle Jimmy went back into printing. He said he was getting too old for wheeler dealing. Sid was always at the race track. He was a gambling man and always on a Saturday you'd find him at Catford greyhound stadium. I had never been. One Saturday afternoon when he was in one of his more amiable moods he said I could go with him. I was given strict instructions – no betting on the dogs.

"It's a mug's game," Mum said. Her motto was, "Neither a borrower nor a gambler be."

Being a first timer, I was in awe of everything I saw. The atmosphere was electric. People were standing right by the trackside waiting to see the action. Upstairs, they were eating and drinking in the galleried restaurant from which you could look down and see the race if you chose not to get caught up in the crowds by the track. A couple of unpleasant-looking gents tipped their hats in recognition when they saw Sid. He seemed to know them, but they didn't speak, just turned their backs on him and walked away. "You don't want to get involved with them," Sid said. "They're trouble."

Sid had several bets running on each race, so we got as close to the finishing line as we could. Sid said, "It's the most exciting place to stand and watch."

The first race consisted of six dogs who were waiting impatiently in the stands. They were the ugliest dogs I'd ever seen, mostly grey in colour with pointed noses and large muscular frames. They had no fur and looked they had been skinned. "They're built for racing, not for beauty," Sid said.

They released the electric hare. It raced round the track at a speed so fast I could hardly follow it with my eyes. The dogs poised, eager and ready to leap out of the stand and run. The gates opened as the hare passed in front of them; they jumped forward spontaneously, following in hot pursuit in the hope that one of them would overtake and capture it and tear it into pieces. The cries from the crowd were deafening. People were shouting the name of the dog that was on their betting slip over and over again. They waved them frantically above their heads in the hope that their dog would be the one romping home in first place and they could claim a prize. I was hooked. From that moment on, I decided I wanted a racing dog. Sid said he'd go halves with me. Me mum said, "Don't think it's coming in the house!"

We scoured the sporting magazines, looking for dogs for sale. Sid said he knew a kennel where we could keep it. With the little bit of savings I had put by and Sid finding the rest of the money, we found a dog for sale. The only problem was, he was coming from Ireland and being a young dog, with a winning pedigree, they were asking a lot of money. Sid said, "To win big, you have to buy big." So he borrowed the additional money we needed, where from I wasn't really sure, and didn't like to ask. We'd seen the picture of this magnificent black dog, Merry Challenge. Sid said, "Just by looking at him you can tell he's a winner." We couldn't wait to pick him up from the ferry port.

We met the chap in a pub in Dover. We drove down in a van we'd borrowed from Dad. We'd already paid for the dog, because otherwise they wouldn't have sent him. A short stocky man in a white overall and check peaked cap met us in the Red Lion pub car park. He was holding on a lead a large, muzzled, angry-looking black dog which lunged aggressively at passers-by and looked like he would tear you to pieces if released from his lead. At that moment, I had second thoughts. The short little gentleman piped up in a very broad Irish accent, "You the Kelly brothers?"

Sid nodded and with that gesture of confirmation the man handed me the leash. "You've bought yourselves a dog, boys. Hope he's a winner for you." He turned round, smiling broadly, then went back into the pub to finish his pint.

"I'm not sitting in the back with him," I said. "He looks a vicious thing." Sid opened the door of the van, tentatively manoeuvring the growling dog nervously inside. I swear to this day if Merry Challenge had not been wearing a muzzle he would have bitten Sid's hand off.

It was an expensive hobby, keeping Merry Challenge; having to pay for his kennelling and training was keeping us skint. Sid, in order to keep up his lavish lifestyle, was borrowing heavily. What a disappointment the dog turned out. I invested all my savings in him. We entered Merry Challenge for every race possible. We travelled all round the country. He was indeed a challenge. Always late out the stands, finishing last every time. The excitement of owning Merry Challenge had now worn off and Sid was in a great deal of debt. We decided that we'd better sell him before he cost us any more money. We advertised him in the *Sporting Gazette*. We had one enquiry to the advert, Merry Challenge never having won a race. He was such a bad-tempered dog we were only offered half the price we paid for him Sid said, "Let's take the money and run."

So we took the money thinking we'd worked a blinder and ran. We still went to the track, and still had the *Racing News* delivered. So we just could not believe it when we read in the paper the following week that Merry Challenge had won the Evening Standard Cup at Wembley. One of the most important events in sporting circles with the largest money prize in dog racing. We could have cried. There was a double page spread in the sporting section of the *Daily Mail* showing a photograph of him with his new owner.

He was smiling broadly, holding the shining silver cup in one hand and a big fat cheque in the other. They retired him after that and he became a stud dog, earning a fortune. There was no point in racing him again as he had reached the top of his career winning the Evening Standard Cup, the most prestigious race there was. I gave up racing after that and never went back to the track. I didn't have the heart. Sid had got himself into deep trouble, unbeknown to the family. He had borrowed extensively to buy his half of Merry Challenge. He bet large sums of money on the dog and even when he continued to lose, betting on him repeatedly, waiting for his winning streak. I was careful, never betting more than I could afford. Sid started to drink heavily. He would come home night after night blind drunk. He couldn't even put his key in the door to let himself in. Dad and Uncle Jimmy tried to have words with him, but being a big lad he took no notice of anyone, least of all Dad. Sometimes he would even raise his fists. Dad always backed down and walked away, not wishing to fight.

Sid and I still shared the attic room. Although Mum had put another bed in there and it was not so unbearable. Sid took to borrowing money off me and I knew he was struggling to pay off the loan he had with the Skinner brothers who, if you didn't pay on time, would break your legs and threaten your family. I took to hiding my wage packet. I often found it gone with no apology or explanation. Sometimes he would threaten me mum and take money from her purse. If she refused, he'd give her a black eye.

It was eleven o'clock Saturday evening. Me mum was worried because Sid wasn't home. Mum kept saying to me, "He's a good boy really. He's just got himself in a little bother." Twelve o'clock came and went. Mum waited up. Sally was on holiday, staying with the Hearts in Ascot, visiting Molly and her new baby. I had gone to bed. There was a loud knocking on the door. Mum was terrified because it was so late, but answered it anyway. On the step was the local constabulary officer. Mum thought she was going to pass out, thinking he was going to tell her that Sid was dead.

He began with, "I must regret to inform you," he removed his helmet, "your son is in a bit of a bad way."

Chapter 30

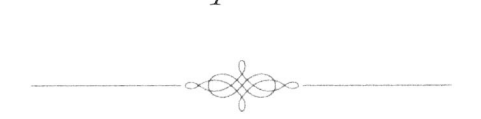

Sid was worried. The roar of the crowd as Hello Dolly came in first made his heart sink to his boots. That was another pony he'd lost on the dogs. He crumpled his betting slip up and threw it onto the floor and made his way to the bar. He had enough money for one more drink and a small bet; he ordered a large whisky, then swirling it round in his glass, he drank it down in one large gulp then looked at his watch and realised it was ten thirty. He was late making his payment to the Skinner brothers. He walked over to the bookie to place his bet. He just knew he was in for a big win. The instalment on the loan he had taken out to buy Merry Challenge had to be paid that day. He'd have one more bet. He was short of a ton to pay the Skinner brothers and they'd already been looking for him earlier in the evening, asking some of the touts if they'd seen him. How he was going to pay them this week, he didn't know. Bob had taken to hiding his wage packet and Mum wasn't bringing any spare money in, and Uncle Jimmy had threatened him and said he'd kill him if he took any more money from her purse without her knowing. He looked through the list of runners. Be Lucky? Perhaps that was a sign, or was it an omen? He wasn't sure. This was his last chance.

He went to stand by the finishing line. They released the electric lure. It went round the track closely followed by all the runners except Be Lucky who was at the back of the field. The race was over in minutes. He was not going to be in the money this time. He turned round and walked away from the track with the face of a loser. Crumpling the betting slip up, he put it in the bin and made his way to find his car. It was dark, the car park was empty of any potential eyewitnesses.

As he put the key in the Ford Capri's door he felt a firm grip on his shoulder.

Without turning round, he knew from the overpowering smell of cheap aftershave that it was Jo Skinner. "Where's our money, Sid?"

Sid tried to release himself from Jo's grip. "Ain't got it, Jo. You've got to give me more time."

"We ain't a bloody charity, Sid," Frankie Skinner said, getting hold of Sid's other arm. He tried to break free, so he could run for it, but he was no match for the two brothers who secured his arms tightly behind his back and put a hood over his head. Then, looking from right to left, making quite sure that the coast was clear of inquisitive onlookers, they pushed Sid into the boot of the car and drove to a small lockup garage beneath the railway arches on the outskirts of Millwall Docks.

The brothers called this their office. The Skinner brothers were like the London Mafia; they were unscrupulous, mean, violent, and unforgiving with no hearts. Their reputation, made people avoid them. Sid had stupidly borrowed extensively from them without any hope of paying them back. With their exorbitant interest rates, it made it impossible for Sid to ever pay off his debt. They had Sid in their pocket. The brothers removed the hood. Then, each taking their turn, hit him, holding him down, punching him again and again. Until Sid, unable to stand, fell to his knees, silently enduring the excruciating pain as his ribs were broken and his face battered beyond all recognition.

The brothers then bundled Sid into the car, drove him to the alley at the back of the Green Man pub in Blackheath, and attempted to undo the ties around

Sid's wrists with a small sheath knife, with the intention of cutting him free and letting him go. Sid, by this time had recovered some of his senses. He attempted to grab the knife out of Jo's hand. They fought hard. Sid was tired and with the severe beating that he had undergone it made him totally incapable of gaining the upper hand against the thickset ex-con who used to be the junior boxing champion. Jo thrust the knife as hard as it would go; it penetrated Sid's leather jacket. Sid felt the knife go deep into his chest. Unable to breathe, he lost consciousness. It was the last thing he remembered before he woke up in Lewisham hospital with Dad standing over him and Mum saying in between her sobs, "What trouble are you going to bring home next, Sid?"

Chapter 31

When he recovered he told people he'd got his wounds as a Navy Seal. I thought this very funny, because I didn't know he could even swim. Luckily enough, which later on proved to save his life, Dad had taught him when he was small, when he'd taken Sid, me, and Mum for our one and only holiday to Morecambe. I can't say I remember it much.

Sid had been found that night by one of the barmen from the pub, the Green Man. His legs had been broken, his face had been battered, and he had a stab wound to the chest. They were not sure if he would survive. He had been taken to Lewisham hospital. Me mum called Uncle Jimmy, and me dad from the phone box up the road and then Dad came and picked us all up in the car and then drove us to see Sid. He was bad, but luckily the stab wound had missed all his major organs. It had been the Skinner brothers. Sid had failed to make his weekly payment.

Dad and Uncle Jimmy said enough was enough, so they clubbed together and paid off Sid's debt. When Sid was well enough Dad took him to the local army recruiting office, where he made sure Sid signed up. Dad said that he was best off out their way for a few years.

He went for the medical and they accepted him for military service. Sid was dead against joining but me dad was having none of it. Mum didn't want him to go, but she knew that he was getting into too much trouble and so she thought in the end perhaps it would be safer. Mum packed his bags and we all went to see him off at the station. Sally's best friend Joy, who she'd met at evening classes studying cookery, asked if she could write to him. I didn't like to say to her she had about as much chance getting a letter back from Sid as pigs might fly but I kept that to myself.

Me mum cried when the train pulled out the station. Dad said, "Don't get upset, Ma. He's only going to Southampton." I was glad I wasn't going too. Joy ran after the train along the platform waving her hanky, but by this time Sid had sat down in the carriage. Dad said, "Typical of Sid. No thought to others." Peace reigned in the household for a little while.

Sid sat down in the train with a feeling of utter relief. He was glad to be leaving Blackheath and the family behind, and Sally's friend Joy. Well, she had become an inconvenience to say the least. Always pestering him, trying to make him give up smoking and gambling. She was only meant to be a bit of fun. One night of fun looked like it was going to lead to a lifetime of nagging and domesticity. That certainly wasn't going to happen to him. Still, he was in the army now, so he had better make the best of it. He knew it couldn't be as bad as Garndiffaith. He was to start his basic army training the very next day.

On his arrival he was allocated a bed so he put away his kit, then lay down and drifted off to sleep. The next morning a very loud, red-faced, aggressive bald man wearing a sergeant's uniform, prodding him constantly with a baton, woke him. For one awful moment Sid thought he was back in Wales and Evan flashed before his eyes. From that moment on, his life became a mixture of intense strenuous physical exercises, gruelling cross countries, serious combat and rifle training, with long and boring lectures on the art of warfare. Followed by evenings of boot polishing and early-morning kit inspections before breakfast. Sid hated it. He was very much a loner. He had no friends to speak of and gained himself a bit of a reputation as being aggressive as he often picked fights over money. He was often found cheating in one of the many illegal card games that took place.

If as much as a button was out of place, or a boot went unpolished, you would be shouted at from dawn to dusk. Sid, however, had a very strong personality and constitution and managed to take the military regime in his stride. A couple of the younger boys teamed up with Sid for his protection. They liked the way he stood up for himself. Gordon and Smithy were the two and Sid didn't seem to mind them hanging around, he enjoyed their admiration. The boys had the evening off. They were given strict instructions to report back to base by ten o'clock. The three of them decided to go to the local pub which was two miles down the road. Sid, Gordon, and Smithy, they weren't what you called friends, but Sid tolerated them. It was dark by the time they were driving back from the pub. Smithy had not been drinking because he knew one of them was going to have to drive. They were late, so rather than taking the direct route back to the barracks Smithy decided to take a short cut through the ford; this would take a few minutes off their journey. None of them wanted to be on a charge. Home leave was coming up and they all wanted home, that was except Sid. Dad had written to Sid telling him Joy was in the family way, and the thought of being saddled with that plain Jane, as obliging as she had been over the sex, left him cold.

It had rained continuously. More than a month's rain had fallen in just one day. The river was swollen; the ground, already saturated, was beginning to flood the neighbouring farmland. They were chatting and laughing as they approached the crossing at the river and for a brief moment Smithy, seeing how high and fast-flowing the water was, nearly decided to turn round. Sid, in his usual bolshie manner, put his hand on Smithy's shoulder and said, "Go for it." That was the last time he was to see Smithy and poor Gordon alive.

Smithy pressed his foot onto the accelerator and the Land Rover hit the water flying, its wheels never even touching the river bed. It swirled round and round in the water, being carried downstream at an alarming speed. The water was already starting to creep inside and circle round their feet. The boys were now panicking, not knowing whether to stay with the car or abandon it to try and beat the dangerous fast-flowing water and attempt to swim to the bank. Sid, without a moment's thought, with all his strength, smashed the window, climbed out, and propelled himself into the water. It felt like he had jumped into a glass of lemonade that had been shaken and had started fizzing and bubbling, gushing over the side with the bubbles going up his nose so that he could not breathe.

It was a powerful spinning current and it took all his capabilities to swim against it to the safety of the bank. He lay there for a while, disorientated. Then, standing up, looking into the distance, he could see the Land Rover bobbing up and down, being pulled along by the powerful current, heading treacherously towards a vertical drop where the water flowed over steep rocks. His last sighting of Smithy was his hand waving frantically out of the window and hearing his desperate, repeated call for help. The young soldiers' battered bodies were recovered from the water three days later. Sid was put on a course of antidepressants, because of the recurring nightmares he was to endure for the remainder of his life.

He would hear Smithy calling out again and again for help.

With the arrival of Dad's letter, which in no uncertain terms told him to return home immediately, he was given compassionate leave. Me mum certainly didn't want no bastards in the family and the neighbours talking behind her back. So much to Sid's reluctance, he returned home to get married. He never mentioned the accident, but it was to bear heavily on his mind, the death of Smithy and poor Gordon, always blaming himself for encouraging the boys to cross the river that night; he could not forget it easily. It played on his mind constantly. He drank heavily to try and block it from his memory. He took pills to take away the voices which he heard constantly. These voices eventually led him to his own destruction.

Chapter 32

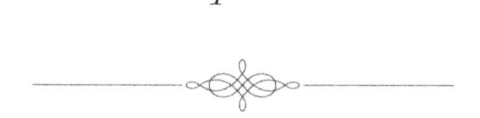

Me mum was cross that Sid hadn't written but he never was good at spelling so writing anything was difficult for him. Uncle Jimmy said it was because he skipped school all the time. Dad said it wouldn't matter in the army as long as he could hold a rifle. I just thought what a dangerous combination, Sid having a rifle. I now had the attic all to myself. The old bed seemed enormous and I slept well for the first time in years, not having to listen to Sid snoring. Sally actually used to get a hot bath in the mornings and Mum didn't have to hide her purse anymore, and there was laughter round the house again.

Uncle Jimmy and Dad, who had built up quite a friendship over the years, used to go for a pint every Friday night at the Coach and Horses in Blackheath village. It was a bit of a rough pub so Mum and Phyllis didn't go. Over the years, Mum had not forgiven Phyllis but had learnt that what you couldn't change you just had to accept and Dad had always been good to us, especially during the war.

Mum used to put her feet up Friday nights and watch the television with a pint of Guinness. It was her tonic, she said. The doctor had told her so.

Me, I just went up the Pally with Harry and tried to pick up girls. Phyllis wasn't a drinker but sometimes she might have a Babycham or Snowball on the nights Dad went out. She said it made her feel like an independent woman. Sally and Joy seemed to have developed a real friendship. They were always together, a bit like me mum and Phyllis were when they were young. What me mum hadn't bargained for was that Sid had left behind a surprise package, and when Sally and Joy came round the Friday before Christmas, Joy had was extremely upset. Sid hadn't written. In fact, nobody was really sure where he was.

Joy was five months gone and it was too late, as me mum said, to do anything about it. So we all decided Joy would move in with us. She didn't have any family of her own and as she was not coping very well with her condition. Sally and me mum said they'd look after her. Joy was poorly all the way through the pregnancy. She was always off work and nobody could ever get in the bathroom in the mornings. Why she was ever called Joy, Mum said, she didn't know. She was such a disagreeable girl and wasn't even pretty. Sid got leave just the once. He seemed to have filled out and put on a bit of weight but he looked good in his uniform.

They were married very quietly in the local registry office. Everyone said it would be the making of him, being a father. I just hoped it didn't turn out like him. They didn't have a honeymoon or a wedding cake. Mum made a suit for Joy and the something borrowed were the little pearl buttons she'd worn on her wedding dress. When I look back at the photos everybody looked sad.

Sid went back the next day to barracks. He didn't say much while he was home, just drank a lot. I was glad to see him go. Uncle Jimmy said he didn't know why he'd even bothered to come home.

Little Charlene was born two weeks premature. Joy had to be rushed into hospital. She called out to Mum from the attic in the middle of the night and said the baby was coming. Everybody panicked. Joy was crying and asking for Sid and we couldn't get him to come home. Even Mum said that she was better off without him there, saying men were no use at times like these.

We had a terrible rush to get to the hospital in time. All the traffic lights seemed to be red, and Joy was screaming blue murder in the back of the car all the way to maternity. Uncle Jimmy drove like a racing driver and we got stopped by the police for speeding. When they knew there was a baby about to be born, they turned on their blue light and gave us an escort all the way. We all felt very important. Mum said she just felt embarrassed, like she was a criminal.

"It was touch and go," the doctor said. Baby Charlene was so tiny and had to be kept in intensive care for over a week. Sid was told he'd got a daughter but he didn't come home and said he'd wanted a son. Joy was very ill after the birth and got septicaemia. They had used the forceps and she got an infection. She died three weeks to the day, after giving birth. When she knew she wasn't going to see Sid, she died heartbroken; he'd never even held his baby girl. He'd said he couldn't get leave. Joy said to me mum he would rot in hell. Little did we know at the time, not a truer word was spoken. Sally said she'd look after Charlene as if she was her own. Sid didn't even come home for the funeral. He showed no interest in his little girl at all.

Me mum doted on little Charlene; we had her christened immediately after the funeral. The vicar said it would be cheaper. Two for the price of one. Mum said, "Sidney wasn't much of a girl's name and as Charlie was Sid's middle name we'd call her Charlene Joy. Joy obviously after her mother."

Me Mum thought it sounded posh and just hoped it bought her more happiness than her poor mother had got from her own life. Sid was sent to Germany for the remainder of his army career and we never saw him again till three years later when he was discharged from the army on medical grounds due to his drug addiction. It caused severe depression. He had always been violent, but the army had changed him and not for the better. Now we felt unsafe in his company, so Dad banned him from the house. I no longer recognised him as my brother.

Chapter 33

Sally had now finished her secretarial course at college, and went to work for a large bank in the city. She spoke very posh, learnt from when she was evacuated with Mr and Mrs Heart. Mum used to get upset because she never brought any friends home and she used to say to Sally that she was ashamed of us all. Sally would catch the train every morning from Blackheath station. She was very eye catching with her flaming red hair and her very high heels that she could hardly walk in. Dad had bought Sally a little black briefcase which she would always carry. It made her look very professional, although anyone who really knew her used to smile because she only had her sandwiches in it. The same people would be on the train every morning and if she was late there was a certain young bloke who would always save her a seat. He was good looking, with a cheeky smile and flirty manner. Michael James was his name. He caught the train further down the line at Chislehurst station. This was a very posh place because Sally had once seen it in the magazine *Home and Garden* and had admired the big Georgian houses that were for sale in the adverts.

"I'll live there one day," she'd said to Mum.

Mum said, "It's where the toffs live," and she should be happy with what she had. She was always coming out with these words of wisdom, none of which she ever took heed of herself, so it always made us laugh. Sally was late that morning and ran for the seven thirty train to Victoria as if she were an Olympic sprinter. Young Charlene had been difficult, didn't want to eat her breakfast and had put everybody behind schedule, screaming and throwing her porridge in all directions, some of which had landed on Sally's suit, so she had to change.

She charged, out of breath, along the platform hoping she might just catch the train before it left the station. Michael opened the door of the carriage and yelled at her to hurry up. He just managed to grasp hold of her arm as the train began to pull away and leave. Sally made one final leap into the carriage. In doing so one of her high heels fell off her foot and disappeared in between the platform and the train onto the tracks. Michael pulled her in to the safety of the carriage and shut the door. Much to everyone's amusement, Sally had to sit for the remainder of the journey wearing just one stiletto. She was so embarrassed. Michael, suggested they took a cab to Selfridges and he would buy another pair of shoes for her. Sally limped on one bare foot through the store and received some very strange looks from the shop assistants. Walking through the departments, she was amazed at the different selection of merchandise they sold.

She kept stopping and admiring everything, like a child visiting Santa for the first time. There seemed to be something from every part of the world. A food department with the strangest cheeses, some of which she had never heard of. A pet department that sold lion cubs and exotic lizards. Makeup, so expensive she could not believe anyone put it on their face and a shoe department displaying the most expensive shoes she had ever seen in her entire life. Sally knew under normal circumstances she would never be able to afford them. The most exquisite pair of red leather shoes leapt out at her and said, "Buy me!" They were pointed with a very high heel, in the brightest ruby red, fashioned out of the softest leather, and on the toe was a sparkling diamante buckle. Sally tried them on focusing her gaze on Michael with the appealing look of a child who wants something they are not allowed to have. Michael was unable to resist Sally's pleading look which he found quite adorable, so he bought them. Sally had never owned a pair of expensive shoes before and in her excitement hugged him with great exuberance.

Looking at herself in the mirror she said to Michael, "They were so glamorous," she felt like a film star. Impressed with his generosity she arranged to meet him that evening for a drink before they caught the train home. It became a regular weekly meeting. Drinks turned into dinner, dinner became romantic liaisons in the bijou little hotel 'The Chocolate Box' two minutes away from Victoria station. The porter became very familiar with them and laughingly called them Mr and Mrs Lovebird thinking to himself Sally with her flaming red hair looked like a bird of Paradise and he wouldn't mind if she was his bird, although he knew with a posh lass like her there wasn't much chance of that. Sally was in heaven, but Michael never gave much away about himself. Sally always described him to mum as deep, dark and interesting, but even though she thought Michael was serious about her, he wouldn't commit himself. He was difficult and evasive, shrugging off any talk of marriage or engagements and wouldn't meet Mum or Dad. He wasn't ready for marriage just yet.

Sally knew he worked for an insurance company and was earning a good wage, he'd often buy her a gift of perfume or flowers, but never what she wanted - the wedding band- her hints always falling on deaf ears.

They had been seeing each other for just over a year, when the relationship came to an untimely end. Sally had never been invited to his home. They always met in London. It was his birthday, he let it slip he wouldn't be able to see her the following week. He was going away on business. Sally, thought she would give him a surprise before he went. But unfortunately for Sally it was her who had the surprise. Wearing a big smile the sexy red shoes and very little else under her coat. Sally knocked on the front door of the very neat looking semi detached house. It wasn't even detached, disappointed she thought it might have been posher, from the way Michael had spoken about it. There was no signs of any workmen or scaffolding for that matter, or the mess that he constantly complained about, or the extension that was in the process of being built, which made it impossible for him to entertain her at his home.

In fact everything was very tidy. Sally rang the bell, wondering if perhaps she was at the wrong house.

After a few moments the door opened. A very pretty young woman who looked no older than eighteen came to the door. Suckling in her arms was a new born baby. "Hallo can 1 help you? My husband isn't here at the moment, he'll be back shortly. He's just popped out to fetch me some groceries. As you can see I've just had a baby. Are you by any chance a work colleague? How nice of you to call."

Hearing the sound of a car pull up behind her Sally turned round to see a sporty little open-top silver Mercedes. Michael clambered out the car and started to walk up the drive in his hands a full bag of shopping out of the top which protruded a box of nappies, he stopped short when he saw Sally, then shrugging his shoulders with an apologetic half smile on his face watched her as she marched angrily past him and disappeared up the road. Putting down the shopping he kissed his wife on the cheek. "What a peculiar girl," he said. "Must have had the wrong house." Taking the little boy from his mother's arms he cooed quietly into his ear whispering, "Never mind, there's always the new secretary in the typing pool."

Sally returned to the station and caught the train back home. She never caught the seven thirty from Blackheath to Victoria again in the morning, but left home much earlier, making sure she always had enough time for the seven o'clock instead. This way she managed to avoid Michael and never saw him again. Michael never tried to get back in touch with her, knowing full well he had outstayed his welcome.

When Sally eventually revealed to me mum why she was so unhappy, me mum said all men were the same and were ruled by their pencil, and hoped she'd learnt her lesson. Sally took a long time to get over it, and it wasn't until she met Arthur later on in life that she settled down. By this time, Charlene was nearly six and had started school.

Chapter 34

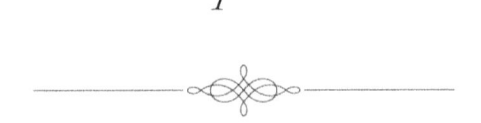

Jimmy was woken up by Connie snoring. It must have been about 4.30 in the morning, but he was awake now and would find it difficult to get back to sleep. He climbed from the bed awkwardly, lifting the covers carefully so that he wouldn't wake Connie. He manoeuvred himself slowly out of the bed. Looking at Connie, he laughed to himself; she always insisted she didn't snore but, every so often, he could hear the break in her breathing and the grunting which sounded like a small piglet snuffling for food. In the early morning light he could see the first signs of grey appearing around her hairline and the small lines that had begun to show around her eyes. These, however, he loved. They creased up when she smiled, although that had not been too much over the last few years.

He considered himself a fortunate man to have Connie and the children. His first sighting of her was at the Ally Pally. Connie had danced with Bert nearly all night and he hadn't got a look in. She was stunning, he had not been able to take his eyes off her. He had been right envious, instead he'd been stuck with Phyllis. An old cow, she was; he'd dated her for a few weeks. He never knew what Bert saw in her but she was too posh for the likes of him, too demanding and wanted too much of the material things in life. He was just a happy-go-lucky sort of chap – a wheeler dealer, his old mum had called him. He had wanted to be a boxer but his dad had broken his arm in three places. They put a pin in it, but he was told he'd never box again, professional or otherwise.

He was glad when the boys had returned home. He hadn't wanted them to go to Wales. But it hadn't been his choice. Sid had come back more difficult than before. He'd tried to help the boy by taking him to work with him, but he knew there was something mentally wrong with him, but Connie would have none of it, and because it wasn't his son he had to sit on the sideline and watch him go down the road to self-destruction. In the end, he didn't interfere. Little Bob, however, he loved like his own, had wanted to make a boxer out of him, but Bob didn't have that killer instinct in him so that went by the way. Sally, he never really had much to do with. He never was great with the girls. He was glad Connie had eventually found out about Bert and Phyllis. Everybody had known except her. He had loved her from the first moment he set eyes on her and was only too willing to step in and help her pick up the pieces of her life.

It had been a long time before she had let him move in. She finally agreed when he and Bert brought the boys back from Wales and they had given Evan that beating for mistreating them so badly.

When the war had come to an end he had been very relieved. Thank the lord he'd managed to get out of enlisting. He'd written regularly to the war office saying that he had to look after his old mum and she was dependant on him. Luckily, she had hung onto the end of the war before she'd sadly passed away, and by the time his call-up papers had come, the war was over.

Having earnt his living buying and selling, he had good contacts in the docks. They used to slip some of the boxes off the pallets when customs weren't looking. He was never sure what was going to be in them until they were opened. It was the nylons he made the most money on. His friend Pete had a stall in the East End on which he used to offload a lot of his stock. Pete and him were always ducking and diving, trying to avoid the local coppers who always had their eyes open, looking for anything that was being sold on the black market. Keeping his slate clean and his nose out of trouble had been quite an achievement. When Bert had packed Sid off to the army, Connie had been quite upset. However, peace had been restored to the house for a little while, and life seem to resume to normal.

Jimmy had been weary of all the arguments. The money that was always missing from Connie's purse and her nearly always in tears. It had been a terrible shame about young Joy, but little Charlene, what a cracker she was. It had been strange having a baby in the house but it sort of brought them altogether. It made them realise how fragile life could be – here one minute, gone the next. Sally had got herself fixed up, she'd been to college and now had a good job in a bank, and Bob had gone back to work with his dad at Bert's Empire. He was now getting too old for standing on street corners selling things out of suitcases. He had gone back to printing. Now working on the local newspaper. It was an early start. But at least he knew where his next pay packet was coming from and he didn't have to be always looking over his shoulder waiting for the strong arm of the law to come to come down on him. He leant over and kissed Connie goodbye before dressing and going downstairs. Connie grunted an acknowledgement then turned over and went back to sleep. She just couldn't cope with early-morning starts anymore.

When Connie died, Jimmy thought his world had ended. The funeral had been arranged by Bob, which Bert had insisted on paying for. Sally had given a speech saying how she had been the best mum and through all her trials and tribulations, had always gone without and always put the children first before herself. She read a poem called 'Our Mum' which brought tears to people's eyes because it struck a chord in everyone's heart.

Phyllis never went to the funeral; Jimmy was glad, he hadn't wanted to see again after their difficult parting all those years ago when he'd call her a money-grabbing bitch. Bert had appeared thoroughly miserable throughout the service. He sat with his head in his hands and everyone knew he silently regretted all the mistakes he'd made and wished things had turned out differently. Jimmy just sat and cried for the loss of his best mate who had been his first love and was now his last.

OUR MUM

Our mum who brought love and laughter
Who fought so hard for us in life
We forgot our troubles and the strife
She fed and clothed us through the barren years
Never questioned, never condemned
Always encouraged the paths we took
Her life was just an open book
Filled with love for all us kids
Our mum who will be so sadly missed
She would always listen to your tales of woe
Put them into perspective so they would go
Pat you on the back and say you'll live to fight another day
She'd make you giggle with her funny quotes
We'd laugh until our tummies ached
Our mum today who's gone away
Who's joined the angels this sad day
We give you Mum your final kiss
Our dearest mum that we all miss.
Around the house although you're gone

We will hear your laughter ring
We know you'll still look after us.
And to us kids the love you bring
Will guide us through the days to come
In times of trouble that life turns up
"Don't worry, luvs," once more you'll say,
"You'll live to fight another day."

Chapter 35

Me mum had suffered terribly worrying over Sid. He was a changed person. He couldn't hold down a job and he took to shouting at people in the street. Me dad seemed to think he was shell-shocked. But as far as I knew he had not seen any active service. Mum said the army must have given him some of those experimental drugs and that's why he had gone all peculiar. He had a small army pension and the council gave him a flat in Sydenham where he lived on benefits. Sally and I used to go and visit him but in the end, we stopped. He was never pleased to see us and Sally was always frightened of him. He was always drunk when we went and the flat was filthy and smelled of smoke.

Sally was doing really well for herself. The Hearts, when they died, left her and Molly a small legacy. Most of the estate had gone in debts and death duties, but they never forgot the pleasure that the two girls had given them. With the money, Sally bought a detached three-bedroom house in Hither Green and Mum and Jimmy, who were elderly and finding it hard to get around, had gone to live with her. Mum was the happiest during that time I'd ever seen her. Sally had all the modern appliances fitted but Mum never did understand the washing machine and how it worked. Sally would come home and Mum would have her sleeves rolled up with all the washing in the sink doing it by hand, no matter how many times Sally showed her how to use it.

Connie was sixty-seven when she died; she was feeling unwell and had been losing weight over the last few months of her life. Mum never complained and never once missed cooking Sally's breakfast for her before she went to work.

We took her to Hither Green hospital to find out what was wrong.

We said, "Goodnight Mum."

Mum said, "See you in the morning, luvs."

When we went back the next day, mother's bed was empty, and they just said to us, "Sorry, your mum died in the night."

We couldn't believe it. We gave me mum a lovely

send-off. All the street turned up. She was well liked by everyone. She always had something to say about everything and was always right. And always saw the funny side of things. Dad came to the funeral and Uncle Jimmy sobbed all the way to the service. He'd really loved me mum. We were glad Phyllis never came, not even to the crematorium. She was unwell at the time. But I don't think me mum would have wanted her there anyway Dad left a beautiful bunch of white lilies on top of the coffin next to Jimmy's single red rose. They were in competition with each other right to the end, Mum would have laughed. Dad's card said, "See you at the Ally Pally. Wait for me. Love Bert." Jimmy's card read, "Save the first dance for me I won't be long." It was me Dad who got the first dance though. He'd been and always was the love of me mum's life, however hard Jimmy had tried. Not long after Dad turned seventy, he went into hospital, the same one where Mum died. He'd had trouble with his breathing and his lungs had filled with fluid and he'd been taken into to have them drained. When I spoke to the doctor, they told me Dad had terminal lung cancer. By the time I'd got back to the ward Dad had died. I felt the same feeling I'd had when we had been left at Blackheath station to be evacuated. Abandoned, thinking I would never to see Dad again.

Dad left Sally some money and me the car lot. He put Sid's money in trust with Sally and me so that he didn't drink it all away, and had asked us to keep an eye on Phyllis. Two days after the funeral I walked down Blackheath Hill with only my memories to keep me company. The day before, the sign above the showroom that had read 'Bert's Empire', had been taken down and as I rounded the corner I could see the new sign had been put up, which read 'Bob's Luxury Cars', and at that moment, although I knew I was completely on my own, I was looking forward to seeing which path life would lead me down, as I was now my own master.

Chapter 36

Sid opened his eyes and yawned. He had not pulled the curtains open yet so there was no natural light, so it was difficult for him to see. The smell of stale cigarettes lingered from the full ashtray that was on the floor beside the bed. Sid ran his tongue round his mouth. It was dry and left him with a bitter, acrid taste. He had not eaten solid food for a few days. Reaching down by the side of the bed, he found the half empty bottle of vodka, the rest he had drunk before falling into bed. Holding the bottle firmly by the neck, he knocked back the remainder of the alcohol. It brought him quickly to reality with a start as the liquor hit his empty stomach, causing him to grimace in pain.

Gathering himself together, he clambered slowly and painfully from the bed. Sid thought, *Good*. Today was Post Office day when he collected his benefit. He was nearly out of cigarettes and booze and that was the only thing that kept him going. Padding across the bedroom floor in his bare feet, he went to the window and opened the curtains to let in the daylight; it made him dizzy, adjusting his vision to the brilliant sunlight that bounced off the dazzling white snow momentarily blinding him. For a second it reminded him of when he was a boy in Wales when he used to snow fight with young Bob in the deep drifts at Garndiffaith and he smiled. What had happened to his family? They'd just given up on him, left him to rot.

The voices he heard in his head, told him they were evil and if he saw them he should kill them. He hated the voices; they never left his head now, making it difficult to sleep without the help of those damn tablets that he would swig down with the booze. He'd received a letter from the council yesterday saying they were going to evict him for non-payment of rent. He was so sure he'd paid, or was Sally meant to be taking care of that? *That bitch of a sister must be keeping Dad's money for herself.*

Perhaps young Bob would help him out. Suddenly there was a loud hammering. Was it coming from his head or from the corridor outside? He heard voices shouting. He couldn't make out what they were saying. He shuffled over to the door; a brown official envelope had been pushed underneath and lay staring up at him from the mat. When everything had quietened down he bent down, picked up the envelope and tore it open. It was an eviction notice giving him twenty-one days to leave. The flats were to be demolished and a new three-bedroom detached house was going to be built on the site. The council had sold him out.

He slumped himself back down in the chair. Where was he to go? He had no friends, no family to talk of. The voices started again in his head. "You've got no one, Sid. You're all alone. No money, no home, no friends. Finish it."

Sid dressed, deliberately not bothering to shave, or wash, lit a cigarette and made his way out of the door and down the stairs. He was a sorry sight, dirty and unkempt and prone to shouting loudly at people in the street. He was carefully avoided by neighbours, who crossed the road when they saw him coming. He walked into the off licence pushed some grubby crumpled notes and the remainder of his loose change from his pocket and demanded a bottle of vodka. The voices constantly talking to him. "Finish it, Sid. Make everybody happy!"

When he arrived back at the flat there was a notice

pinned to the front door in black capital letters. 'Notice of demolition'. Sid ripped it from the door and left it lying on the pathway. Climbing the stairs, he felt weary. He pulled out his keys to open the door and found that he had not even bothered to lock it. Still, the voices muddled around in his head. Opening the bottle of vodka, he sat down in the old brown armchair, reached into his pocket and pulled out a bottle of antidepressants. How many was he supposed to take? He just couldn't remember. He tipped half the bottle into the palm of his hand, tilted his head backwards and swallowed the tablets one by one. He closed his eyes and as he slowly drifted off to sleep, numbed by the vodka. He could hear quite clearly his Mum saying, "You're late again, Sid."

His last words as he reached out to her were, "Sorry Mum, I'm on my way."

He was found two weeks later by the council enforcement officers "Poor sod," they said. "Don't believe he had any relatives."

Neighbours said, "He was mad as a hatter."

He was still sitting in his old brown armchair when he was discovered, then taken away unceremoniously by the council and cremated. No one went to the funeral, and he wasn't even given a headstone. When

Joy had said he would rot in hell on the day Charlene had been born, She turned out to be right.

Chapter 37

Life was good. I knew in which direction I was headed. I wasn't bad looking – according to some I had a look of James Dean about me. The car lot had grown into an impressive showroom for affordable cars. A far cry from the days of Bert's Empire when I cleaned and valeted the old cars that came in that Dad would sell on. No tinkering of the mileage, no rescued crash victims, just genuine family runarounds.

Once a week I visited Sally in her house at Hither Green. I was quite envious of her domestic bliss. She'd met a policeman and finally settled down and married. She would say to me, "I don't want you getting involved with anything illegal, or bringing any trouble home. We've had enough of that with Sid over the years." We'd both given up visiting Sid. He was argumentative when we went and only asked for money. Sally, however, still made sure that he had his monthly income paid into the local post office from Dad's estate. What he did with it, we were never sure, but we had an idea it went on the horses or the dogs.

I never had the heart to bet on another dog after the disastrous experience we had with Merry Challenge, and looking at a greyhound always used to make me feel sick. We had not seen Sid for some time and both felt guilty. He was still our brother, albeit a difficult one. Sid had been diagnosed with schizophrenia and that's when all his problems had started. We had just thought he was a drunk. The time came when I couldn't put off visiting Sid any longer. We had left it too long. I didn't tell Sally I was going. I thought it best, knowing how she would worry.

It was October; the weather was very temperamental. It could be sunny one minute and snowing the next. I gave the old red Jaguar a final polish, then took some money from the petty cash. I thought back over the years. No doubt Sid would ask for cigarettes. Climbing into the car, I turned the key and listened to the low throaty roar of the engine, and paused for a moment, wondering if I was doing the right thing. But before changing my mind I put my foot down on the accelerator, slowly pulling away, filtering the car into the oncoming traffic, and headed in the direction of Sydenham where Sid lived.

Although I had not visited Sid for some time, I knew the drive well. My first girlfriend, Ann, who I'd met at the Pally, lived in Sydenham with her younger sister Brenda and her mum, Rose. I'd fallen head over heels in love with Ann when I had just turned sixteen years of age. To get into the Pally you had to be eighteen, but being quite fit-looking for my age from panel beating the cars, it was easy to slip by the doorman and give the appearance of being older than I was.

Every Friday me and Harry, who both looked all of twenty, would dress in long tailored jackets with velvet collars, grease our hair as high as it would go, and put on our thick rubber-soled dancing shoes, then get on the bus to Sydenham to go rock and rolling, which had become all the craze. The teddy boys had arrived. Ann was nineteen, very slim and extremely nimble and could rock and roll like a professional dancer. It was love. I dated her for quite a few weeks, me thinking this was the one. Harry was extremely jealous; he hadn't found a girlfriend and Ann's younger sister Brenda didn't fancy him. Harry let my little secret out one Friday when he'd got fed up with Ann and me jiving round the floor. He'd run out of money and was fed up with sitting alone. When I'd gone to the bar to get another drink he had made a pass at Ann. Slapping him on the cheek, she said to him, "Bob won't forgive this, Harry. You've acted like a child."

Ann picked up her glass of Babycham and was just about to leave when Harry said to her, "I thought you liked kids, Ann. Bob being only sixteen."

Ann extracted the truth from me later that night. We left separately. The following Friday Ann was seen jitterbugging with her new boyfriend, Johnny Baxter, who was known to be at least twenty as he was on leave from the army. I didn't speak to Harry again for a long time. Turning into Sydenham High Street, I took the third on the left with the grocer's shop on the corner and kerb crawled slowly down the road looking for number 32 Palace Close. I drew up outside, switched off the engine, then lit a cigarette. I was glad Mum wasn't alive to see me smoking. Dear old Mum, she used to say smoking would lead me to an early grave.

Composing myself, I got out of the car and locked the door – you could never be too careful round here. Walking up to the house, I double checked the number on the gate post. It read number 32. I was confused. The house which was divided into two flats, one of which Sid lived in, was boarded up. The garden was completely overgrown and the front door had a notice of impending demolition on it. Where was Sid? I went next door and rang the bell. "Do you know where Sid went?" I asked the old pensioner who had come to the door in her curlers and slippers.

"That old drunk. He died about six months back. Having no relatives, the council came and took him away. They cremated him, his ashes are scattered at Grove Park crematorium. Sad," she said, "to die alone."

I turned round and walked slowly back up the path, tears filling my eyes. I could not believe that no one had tried to contact Sally or myself. Even in death I had not been a brother to him. Getting back into the car, I wondered what I would tell Sally. Driving home, I silently apologised to Mum and wept for the brother that I never really knew. Telling Sally had not been as bad as I thought it would. Grief affects people in many ways. Little Charlene, Sid's daughter, had never known her father and had been told he'd died in active service in the army. It was only years later that she learnt the truth, but she never understood why we'd failed to tell her that Sid was alive. Sally made sure the little bit of income that had been given to Sid each month was put in a savings account for her for when she was older.

Chapter 38

Sally became depressed over Sid's death, blaming herself for not going to see him. Thankfully, her marriage to Arthur was a happy one and although she had not been able to have any children of her own, the house was always filled with laughter due to Charlene. The family never knew the terrible circumstances which stopped Sally being able to have a family. Me mum had kept it a secret, never telling me until just before she died, so that someone would still put flowers on the little boy's grave. Sally never told Arthur either, just said it was women's problems why she couldn't conceive. Arthur said it didn't matter. They had Charlene, didn't they? And that was enough for anyone, as she had the characteristics of her father, Sid, and could be a little difficult at times.

Sally, three weeks after she had ended the affair with Michael James, had found she was in the family way. Dad would have killed the bloke if he had found out, and Mum, well she would have been heartbroken if she'd known at the time. Sally, loving her job as she did, and having just received a promotion, she couldn't have this baby. A friend of hers, Marjorie Simpson, told her about a doctor who lived in Camberwell. Me mum would have been furious if she'd known what Sally had intended.

"A life is a life," Mum would have said. Sally told the family she was going away on business.

Climbing into the cab Sally felt sick wondering in her heart if she was about to make the right choice. Michael, she knew would want nothing to do with another baby, already having a wife and family tucked away in the suburbs. Clasping the piece of paper which had the directions and details that Marjorie had given her earlier in the week, she tapped on the glass partition of the cab. "We're here," she said, telling the cabbie to pull up outside the red bricked house, handing a few coins out of her purse to him, not forgetting the tip.

Climbing slowly out of the taxi, Sally walked hesitantly up the path to the front door. Almost changing her mind, but turned round to see the cab had already disappeared round the corner and was out of sight. She knocked. It was opened immediately by an elderly Indian women wearing a beautiful green silk sari who had been watching intently out of the window for her arrival. Not wanting the young lady caller to draw any unnecessary attention to the house. "You'll be Mrs James," she said. Sally nodded, she had decided not to give the doctor her correct name and address, The Indian lady showed Sally up a dimly lit narrow flight of stairs into a drably decorated waiting room. She smiled bowing and nodding, repeatedly clasping her hands together up and down as if she were about to say a prayer. Looking around Sally realised at one time, the room must have been a child's bedroom - the walls were covered in Muffin the Mule. She sat there and thought how inappropriate and distasteful.

The doctor called her in. The procedure was humiliating, painful, and degrading. Crying a lot, because of what she had done, she handed over the blood money. The doctor told her to go home and lie down and the inevitable would happen. Three hours later, alone in the attic room with a feeling of utter hopelessness, Sally said goodbye to the little foetus that would have been Michael's son. Wrapping him carefully in a blanket, then placing him in a cardboard box, she crept quietly through the house to the fields at the back, dug a shallow grave and buried him next to my beloved Chum. "Guard him safely, Chum," she said. Then with her head bowed walked tearfully back to the house, climbed back up the stairs to the attic and prayed to God to forgive her for what she had just done.

Sally kept her secret. It was only many years later that she told Mum, who when she heard, was inconsolable for the grandchild she would never see. Sally showed Mum where he was buried and after that, Mum placed flowers on the grave every week and prayed for his lost soul. She named the little boy that was never given the chance to grow up Thomas, after her dad Robert Thomas that she'd never known, who had died before she had been born. Although later after Jean's death she'd found out he'd gone off with another woman.

Charlene had grown into a difficult teenager. Sid was her flesh and blood, you could never forget that. Unfortunately not a pretty girl, she had taken on a great likeness to her father. She was wild and unruly. Me mum used to compare her to Cathy out of *Wuthering Heights*, because she was always wandering off on her own. Her hair was jet black and curly like Sid's had been. She would never fasten it in ribbons and always let it fall untidily around her shoulders. Mum used to say that it would change when she became interested in boys. Charlene's saving grace was her wonderful wicked sense of humour. She was always making us laugh and would do wonderful impersonations of us all. At Christmas time, she would dress up and put on a one-man show, singing and dancing, and she would fly across the parlour, leaping and pirouetting as if on a London stage. When she was sixteen, Sally decided to enrol her in the London College of Performing Arts.

Arthur said she was a terrible drama queen, and it would be the ideal occupation for her. We were all a bit nervous, as it was the first time she had ever been away from home.

It would be a very brave person who took on Charlene. Just like Sid at her age, she was ready to take on the world. Student life suited her. She loved the bustle of London life, and just as her father was, terrible at corresponding. At the weekends she would wander around Camden. Wearing an old RAF flying jacket, a pair of faded blue denim jeans with a pair of suede over-the-knee boots, she looked almost boyish in her attire. The nearly new stalls in the market drew her to them and it was not often she would come home without purchasing some incredibly ancient item of clothing that she just had to have.

A year into her course, they had been preparing a show for the end of term, 'Guys and Dolls'. Charlene took one of the leading parts, Sarah Brown. It was a fierce, energetic musical that was to push Charlene's acting, singing, and dancing talents to the foremost. We had all been invited to attend. Sally was horrified when she saw what Charlene had to wear. She thought it was indecent. Arthur said, "That's the theatre for you." We were transported back into a world of gangsters, gambling, and seedy nightclubs. It was hilariously funny. We were enthralled. Charlene danced and sang as if that was what she had been born to do. Sally cried. We were all so proud. Encore after encore was taken, flowers were thrown onto the stage, the whole auditorium stood up and the clapping and shouts of "More! More!" must have been heard in the street outside.

Unbeknown to the school, there had been a talent scout in the audience that night. He approached Charlene after the show had finished and asked her to audition for a major part in a leading West End show, 'You'll be Lucky'.

Later on in the year the whole family went up to London again to see Charlene shine at the famous London Theatre 'The Adelphi' in the Strand. It was the beginning for her of a long and successful career in musical theatre. We often wondered what Joy would have said, if she had been alive. But I reckon she would have been extremely proud. Charlene never married, and Sally and Arthur were denied the pleasure of having a grandchild. Sally often wondered if God was punishing her for what she had done.

I, however, knew otherwise. Years later, on one of my many visits to London shopping with my wife Marilyn, we had caught sight of Charlene, arm in arm, walking down Carnaby Street with a very odd-looking female. All her long, black, curly hair had been cut into a very short bob, which at the time was the latest fashion. She walked with a very masculine stride and she had taken on a very manly persona. Every so often the two girls would stop and kiss, then continue on their way holding hands, looking affectionately at one another.

Needless to say, Marilyn and I never acknowledged them, and we never mentioned it to the family. It was a secret that Marilyn and I kept and Sally and Arthur were never the wiser for it.

Chapter 39

Charlene knew something was up, but nobody would talk to her. She kept hearing Auntie Sally and Uncle Arthur whispering about her dad Sid. Charlene had never known her father. He had died in active service in the Army, that's what Granny Connie had told her anyhow. They had been very proud of him. Uncle Bobby wouldn't talk about her dad at all, which she thought was very strange, but apparently he had been a bit of a wild child. Everybody said she looked like her dad, but nobody ever showed her any photos so she had nothing to compare. Joy, her mum, had died when she was born so she looked on Sally as her mum, although they didn't always see eye to eye, and Sally would say, "You've got your dad's temper and it's not ladylike for a girl to act that way."

From a very early age Charlene knew she was different. She hated dolls, loved to climb trees, and wanted to play with the boys and be with the boys. If Sally made her wear a dress Charlene would always wear a pair of trousers underneath, much to the disappointment of Granny Connie, who said she always looked like one of the Indians from the takeaway up the road.

Bert said, "They might as well take her away as she looks like one of them with her dark skin."

Charlene was very funny; she made us laugh, and often cry at her silly anecdotes. Agile and energetic, and with her slim frame could perform arabesques and grand jete's as if she had been schooled by the Royal Ballet, although she would not be seen dead in a tutu. After Connie and Bert died she became very unsettled and often rebelled against any rules and regulations that Sally tried to put into force. Arthur thought she needed to focus more on a career.

The last Bank Holiday in August we had driven to London to see her in the closing performance of 'You'll be Lucky'. Sally had decided early on that she should live in London and had found her a little bedsit just off Camden high street. it was small but comfortable and cheap. It was a basement flat with its own front door with steps leading down to it from the street, very dark but she didn't seem to mind. She was just excited at her newfound independence. Sally made sure Charlene was given a small allowance from Grandad Bert's will. This paid her rent. She never knew where the money originated from. It was money that had been meant for Sid. Dad had left it to me and Sally's discretion what to do with it, knowing that Sid would have most likely gambled or drank it away. After a tearful goodbye, and false promises to write, we left her to her own devices and returned home.

Chapter 40

Charlene loved the jaded little bedsit. It had begun to get dark, and as it was a basement flat it was quite gloomy, but she found this comforting. She had a bottle of red wine left from the previous night so opened it and poured herself a glass then fell back into the old Queen Anne leather chair. Slipping into a light sleep, she dozed in and out of consciousness. She couldn't relax due to the excitement of her performance that evening. Abruptly being brought back to reality by a loud thumping, it sounded like somebody was about to come through the ceiling, or was dancing with hobnail boots and attempting to do the flamingo. The music was deafening and Charlene knew that she would not be able to sleep with all the commotion. Feeling annoyed, she put on her old blue cardigan, wrapping it tightly around herself, went out of her front door and climbed the steps to the flat above where the noise seemed to be coming from. It was a blustery day and her hair flew wildly in every direction making it difficult for her to see. Attempting to negotiate the slippery concrete steps she missed her footing. Grabbing frantically at fresh air in a clawing comical desperation to regain her balance before she hurdled to the ground, the front door opened and Charlene fell headlong into the arms of a very good looking young man, who trying very hard not to laugh said, "You must be my new neighbour. Do come in."

He was handsome and charming. His name was Giles; he had a slightly feminine way about him when he talked and the way he held his tea cup with his little finger extended made Charlene laugh. It reminded her of Uncle Bob; his finger curled, it had never straightened after an accident when he was a boy. Giles loved rock music and wore the most flamboyant clothes that she had ever seen. Very soon they became inseparable friends, each understanding the other. It came to Charlene very early on in the friendship, although it was never discussed openly, that Giles had a keen interest in young men rather than young women. This, however, never bothered her. At that time, she had not found her true sexuality, and love at that time with a member of the same sex was completely taboo.

Giles was an in-and-out-of-work actor. He was either up or he was down, in love, or desolate. It was a roller coaster of a friendship but Charlene loved the soirees he would have. They would all gather in the top floor flat, drinking wine, discussing politics, that nobody really knew anything about, but it made you seem intelligent. The flat would be filled with young potential Shakespearian actors, all name dropping, all hoping to make it big on stage or screen. It was a gay time. Charlene blossomed from a discontented teenager into a talented young woman, about to discover her true self and make her own way in the world.

Charlene very early on in life, knew that she was drawn to other women. She would have strange flutterings sometimes when a scantily dressed attractive chorus girl would come into the dressing room. She never felt the same excitement that the other girls experienced when glancing through *Spotlight* magazine at the muscular, tanned, budding young actors that leapt out from the pages at you, saying, "I'm available."

Gerry was very petite; her mother was French and her father Chinese. Her parents had met when they had appeared in the stage show, 'Showboat'. They were a strange combination but had fallen instantly for each other and shortly afterwards had produced Gerry. English speaking, with a French accent, slightly yellow skinned with short dark cropped hair, she also was attracted to other women. Charlene and Gerry met at one of Giles' afternoon soirees. Gerry was sitting alone in the corner of the room. She had an important audition coming up the followings day and was repeating the lines to the poem 'The Owl and the Pussycat', over and over again, trying to remember them ready for the next day, desperately wanting a part in the new Noel Coward play, that half of London wanted to appear in.

Charlene took the book from out of Gerry's hands. "Let me help you with your lines," she said. Gerry looked up, and from that moment on they were both lost, and their fate sealed. It was to be a long time before same-sex couples were accepted and Charlene hid this secret nearly all her life. Love blossomed slowly between the two girls and they attempted to keep their relationship hidden from everyone except Giles, who just accepted it as normal. Charlene's career took off with a flourish. She travelled to Broadway and her name was always in the spotlight, prominently illuminated above the theatre, heading the cast, always showing her in the starring role. She didn't come home to see us very often and her lack of interest in correspondence made us liken her to Sid even more.

Charlene and Gerry had not been friends for very long when early one evening as they were leaving the theatre a tall, dark haired scruffy, middle aged man who had been standing outside approached the two girls. On his breath you could smell stale cigarettes and last night's drink. He held out his shaking hands to Charlene and tried to take her arm. "I'm so proud," he said. Charlene was quite frightened for a moment, and for a split second when their eyes met Charlene thought she was looking in a mirror, and looked questioningly at the unkempt man standing in front of her. Gerry pulled her from his grasp and they got into the waiting cab.

As the taxi drew away from the kerb she looked back over her shoulder at the dirty, dishevelled, dejected-looking man standing by the roadside that she had hastily rejected. "Just some old drunk," Gerry said, but in that brief moment of meeting a niggling doubt crept into Charlene's mind and she wondered who he had been.

A few months later she learnt from one of the audience of Sid's death. He was one of the Skinner brothers who lived in Blackheath and had lent Sid money. He had come to wish her well after the show and offer his condolences for her father who had died a few months back. He had really only wanted money cos Sid had owed him a packet which he'd lost to him in a card game. Sid had let slip to Joe Skinner he had a daughter that worked in the theatre . When Charlene eventually found out Sid had been alive all those years. She understood why we had kept him a secret from her , but she really never forgave us, and from that moment cut us out of her life, only sending the odd Birthday card or Christmas card. Much to Sally's heartache and distress because she loved Charlene so dearly.

Charlene visited the crematorium sometimes when she had leave from the theatre and would place flowers there. She would sit on one of the wooden benches and talk to Sid and tell him he was not forgotten and would have been loved if she had only known he had been alive.

But knowing Sid as he had been, I knew that this would not have been possible and that she was completely misguided in her belief that she would ever have been loved, and could have given love, and somehow made Sid whole.

Chapter 41

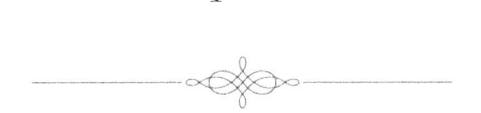

Although Sid and I had not been friends, it felt very strange to no longer have a brother. Working all the time to keep the business going made it difficult for me to meet anyone, male or female, and for a few years after Sid's death I felt very much alone. Sally was busy with her life and her charity work for unmarried mothers. The showroom was stocked full of cars. I had been to the sales and overstretched myself, but I'd just had to put that last bid on the little red Mercedes sports car. She stood right at the front of the showroom and what a looker the car was, already bringing the punters in. I'd polished her and cleaned her inside and out. Standing beside the car was the most gorgeous girl. Long blonde hair down to her waist and a natural beauty about her that certainly didn't come from a bottle. Straightening my tie and clearing my throat, which had now become quite dry, I approached this wonderful feline-like creature who had the longest legs I think I'd ever seen. I approached her nervously. I didn't care if she wanted to buy a car or not. I just had to speak to her.

"Can I help you, miss?" I said, trying to get the words out but nothing seemed to be happening. My brain didn't seem to be connecting with my power of speech.

She turned to me and smiled.

"That's a cockney accent, isn't it? I'd like to buy this car."

At that moment I knew, just like me mum said I would, that this was the girl I was going to marry. "Let me take you for a test drive," I said.

I opened the car door to the passenger seat, and I watched her with admiration as she swung her legs elegantly into the car. Marilyn was her name. Her mother had named her after the film star Marilyn Monroe and boy did she look like a film star. It turned out that she was studying opera at the London School of Music and she had aspirations of being a singer. I wondered then if she was a little too posh for the likes of me, but as me mum used to say, "A standing pencil has no conscience." I never knew what she meant at the time, but I certainly did now. The test drive turned into lunch at an old pub twenty minutes up the Old Kent Road. We never stopped laughing, her at my cockney accent and me at her posh one. I was hooked and couldn't wait to see her again.

Needless to say, she never bought the car, and on that day had no intention of doing so. I was never really sure why she had come into the showroom, but perhaps it was just meant to be. Micky said that she fancied me rotten. I like to believe that, anyway. Her parents never liked me, especially her dad. Like any father who has a daughter, I was not good enough for his Marilyn. She was still at college and they did not want her singing career ruined. We used to sneak away whenever we could to be together. It felt like we were in the throes of having a clandestine affair, not a regular relationship. It made it so exciting. Marilyn, for all her maturity was still very naive about sex, and as much as I tried, she still held back from me.

"I don't want to get pregnant, Bob," she would say.

I resigned myself to the fact unless I was going to marry her, I was not about to pop my cork, as Sid used to do regularly under the bedclothes in the attic when we were boys. I would ask him what he was doing, and he would laugh and say, "I've just popped my cork, Bob. You should try it." It was not till a while afterwards that I understood what he meant.

Marilyn and I had gone for a picnic on the River Thames. We found a secluded spot, not overlooked, a twenty minute walk from the main path. A tranquil setting, where the water lapped gently against the bank, with the over head trees just giving enough shade from the heat of the sun. The peace only broken by the odd duck in the distance having a disagreeable squabble with its mate. It was an ideal spot for a romantic liaison and I had researched it thoroughly before bringing Marilyn there to propose. Unfolding the blanket from the picnic basket, I took out the bottle of champagne and poured two glasses, placing a bowl of succulent wild strawberries and cream alongside them.

"Oh, Bob! You're so romantic," she had said.

I took from my pocket the small ring box that I had purchased earlier in the week from Hatton Garden. The diamond it contained was far more that I could really afford, but I had not wanted her thinking I was mean.

The diamond sparkled in the bright sunlight, and kneeling before her, looking directly into her green twinkling eyes, I had asked her to marry me.

"Yes Bob," she said. "I will."

I took her in my arms and very gently pressed my lips against hers.

"I will always look after you, love," I'd said.

I pushed her down against the blanket, slowly, one by one, undoing the buttons on the front of her blouse. I reached round and unclipped her brassiere revealing her small pert nipples, aroused by the gentle caressing. I entered her slowly at first, then my passion overcame me and we rode together like two young horses wild and free. We lay back, exhausted, side by side, holding hands.

Coming back to reality, my only thought had been, *Oh God, I hope I haven't made her pregnant.*

Marilyn's only thought was Oh God, how was she going to tell her mother and father? Plucking up as much courage as I could, I donned my one and only suit, purchased the biggest bunch of flowers, and made my way over to where Marilyn lived with her mother and father. The house was situated on the posher side of Blackheath bordering the large green. It was five bedrooms arranged over three floors, with stunning views across London. It was very different from the little terraced house that I had been brought up in. Mum would have thought it was a hotel. On entering the house, you walked down a long, narrow, tiled hallway leading into a large open-plan kitchen which was the meeting point in the house, where everybody sat and discussed the day's events over a cup of coffee or an evening meal. Marilyn's parents ushered me inside and sat me down. I offered the bunch of flowers up like a peace offering but they were not acknowledged and were left sadly unattended on the table. Marilyn was nowhere to be seen. her father stood, arms folded, looking at me. Before I could say anything, he glanced across at his wife to acknowledge that they were both in agreement and said, "I'm sorry, Bob. It's not that we don't like you. Marilyn is much too young and has got to finish her studies. She is going to be a great singer."

I knew then I was facing a losing battle. I left the house that day feeling as if my heart had been cut in two. However hard I tried to see Marilyn after that, she was always unavailable. I learnt shortly afterwards that she had been sent to Italy to further her studies. I thought, then I was going to get a passport.

Chapter 42

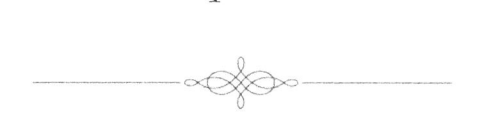

Marilyn saw the car first and thought, *Gosh! what a beauty!* She walked past the showroom at least twice. One day she thought, *I'll own one of those.* The little Mercedes sports car gleamed like a new pin. It was bright red in colour and stood out like a shining star amongst the old family runarounds that were alongside it. No harm, she thought, in just having a look, so biting her lip, straightening her skirt, and holding herself as upright as she could to give herself a feeling of self-importance, she walked into the showroom. The salesman was a bit of alright, she thought to herself. He reminded her of an actor she had seen in the films. Which one, she wasn't sure. He was blond and really quite handsome, and spoke with a really funny cockney accent that she had trouble understanding. Marilyn could tell he was interested in her because of the way he ogled her legs and his eyes looked her up and down in a sort of eager anticipation. Marilyn paused for a moment before accepting the offer of a test drive. Then thinking, *What the heck?* climbed into the little sports car, making quite sure that the young man had enough time to appreciate her exceptionally long legs. Little did she know that this encounter was to determine her whole future and be the start of her whole new life.

Marilyn's parents knew she could sing from a very early age. From the age of three, she would recite poems and sing nursery rhymes. Her voice had the sweetest tone, the neighbours used to say when they came in for drinks at Christmas, when Marilyn was asked to sing for them. Marilyn's parents, Charles and Helen, encouraged her as much as they could.

They gave her singing lessons, piano lessons, and elocution lessons. They went with her to singing competitions and travelled with her all round England. They were determined that she was going to be a big star. Marilyn's favourite genre was opera and she would sit for hours listening over and over again to the records of Maria Callas and Joan Sutherland, and dream of being a famous singer. Every chance she could she would visit the opera, and now after finishing her studies at the London School of Music she was to study in Milan at the Giuseppe Verdi

Conservatory. Falling in love with Bob had not been on her agenda; leaving him had been one of the most difficult things – career or marriage. But her parents gave her no choice. They had supported her all the way, now she must give them back something in return. She just hoped Bob would wait for her.

On her arrival in Italy, she was mesmerised by the culture, the food, the nightlife, and the handsome Italian romantic young men who dressed so elegantly, bought her roses and whispered in her ear the erotic words of love, leaving her breathless and wanting more, but she never could stop thinking of cheerful, kind, cockney Bob, who certainly did have a romantic side, did want to marry her, and had promised to look after her. Bob may not have been the best of dressers. She had an ache in her heart, though, so strong that she would lay in bed at night in her room in the villa that the school used for boarding the students, and she would cry silently, thinking only of her lost love and when she would see him again.

Chapter 43

Marilyn's shoulders hurt from where she had fallen asleep in the sun, and her voice was hoarse from singing. She was quite despondent. Herself and Katerina, a fellow student, had been called into the office that day and had been told as tactfully as possible that they would never make opera singers. Not only were their voices not pure enough, they both lacked the dedication and long-term commitment and suffering that was required of one to reach the pinnacle of becoming a great opera star. After two glasses of red wine over lunch and one final singing lesson, they both agreed they would go home to England. So, in a more jovial mood after promising one another they would always stay friends, they came out of class clinging to each other. "We're off to see the wizard the wonderful wizard, of Oz."

Marilyn suddenly stopped dead in her tracks when

coming face to face with Bob in the corridor. All she could take note of was his out of place Panama hat and the most tasteless white socks and Jesus sandals he was wearing, making him look completely absurd. Looking at his feet as if drawn to them by a magnet, she said, "I can't believe you're wearing Jesus sandals."

Bob laughed. "They were good enough for him," he said, "so they're good enough for me." Then roaring with laughter, they fell into each other's arms.

Chapter 44

I was not about to give up just yet on Marilyn. I knew that her parents had sent her to Italy for further studies. So, enrolling my young friend Micky to look after the car lot, and having made extensive enquiries at the London School of Music as to her whereabouts, I embarked on my rescue mission. Not before applying for my first passport and investing in some new, what I thought, were the latest fashion summer clothes. I found a Panama hat in a tailor shop in Millwall. I thought it made me look distinguished. The assistant let me have it cheap. They said there was not much call for Panama hats in Millwall because of the weather. I purchased my ticket to Milan, and for someone who had never been further than the other side of the river I was looking forward to the adventure I was about to undertake. I could, however, hear me mum's voice in my ears, saying, "You be careful, Bob. All those foreigners. Remember the war."

I found the airport very confusing, never having travelled before. There seemed a whole number of boarding gates of which I had no idea which one to choose. I managed check-in without too much fuss, and settled down in the waiting lounge with a pint of lager and a cheese sandwich.

Sat next to me was another young traveller of a similar age to me. He introduced himself as George; he was also going to Milan, but to an engineering factory in the industrial part of the city. He had taken on a new job there and was flying out to take his position in his father's company. Luckily for me he spoke fluent Italian, which I was very grateful to be able to take advantage of on arrival in Italy. I learnt that I was not a good flyer. On take-off my ears had popped and for the rest of the flight I found it difficult to hear what people were saying. When the air hostess started to demonstrate the crash and lifebelt guidelines I started to panic thinking we were all going into the sea. George, however, was a regular traveller back and forth over the continents, so with a reassuring pat on my back and a large whisky, I was able to control my anxiety for the rest of the flight.

On arrival at Milan airport, I was very glad to have George by my side. He arranged a car and a cheap boarding house for us both. Without him, I possibly would have got on the next flight home.

The boarding house was up a narrow, cobbled side street. How we got there I will never know. The cab driver had driven like a maniac, cursing and swearing round every corner, swerving and beeping his horn every few minutes at the same time shaking his fist and shouting, "Idioti!" at every passing car.

George seemed to think this was normal, but I did not want to repeat the experience again too soon. It was already beginning to get dark, so after a very bad attempt at trying to manoeuvre a plateful of spaghetti into my mouth, much to the amusement of George who was an experienced Italian diner, we then retired for the night.

The room being comfortable but lacking in opulence of any kind, was very hot, so walking across the threadbare carpet, I went to the window to open it. The warm air hit my face and I could hear the sound of young Italians gossiping in the street below, saying, "Buona notte," and kissing each other goodnight before climbing on to their scooters with the sound of the engines starting up and the *pop, pop,*

pop as they made their way over the cobbles back onto the main square.

I climbed into bed, wondering what Marilyn was doing, and fell into an uneasy sleep. Waking early the next morning I was greeted by brilliant sunshine entering the room through a small gap in the curtains and I could hear that the city was already awake and calling me to explore. Dressing in my new clothes, cream shorts, white socks and sandals, popping on my new Panama hat and tilting it slightly to one side, I was under the misguided illusion when I looked in the mirror that it gave me the appearance of a sophisticated young man.

Then, popping on my new Armani designer sunglasses which I had purchased in the duty free, I made my way downstairs and into the busy street, eager to embark on my adventure. The noise was deafening, cars hooting, Italians talking, and scooters coming at you in every direction.

So this was Italy. I had fallen in love. The streets were alive. I could smell the coffee and my taste buds were beginning to salivate for the chocolate croissants that George had told me about.

I dawdled along taking in the sights, the beautiful Italian, olive-skinned girls, who smiled and nodded at me saying, "Buongiorno," as they passed. Then turning to each other, laughing and saying in a whisper, "Inglese," and pointing at my socks and sandals, which didn't appear to be as fashionable as I thought. The Italian young men seemed so elegant in their beautifully tailored trousers and white linen shirts, just open at the neck, enough to reveal a small gold crucifix necklace against their suntanned skin. They looked fashionable and sophisticated, and now looking at my appearance as I caught sight of myself in a shop window, I seemed completely inappropriately dressed, amongst these debonair-looking, charming young Italian men. Their shoes made of the softest leather looked as if they had come from a crocodile farm and appeared they had seen no usage at all. When they smiled, they revealed the whitest teeth, making them look exceedingly attractive and looking at my competition as I walked along, I kept thinking perhaps Marilyn was already lost to me.

Everybody seemed to know each other, and from every corner of the street you could hear Italian being spoken, and see people hugging one another in recognition. I understood now why Italy was the city of romance. Finding a cafe for breakfast was easy. Round the square there must have at least six or seven, the tables all covered in check cloths and shadowed by large brightly coloured parasols, all looking as inviting as one another. I sat down on an empty table, and within seconds a waiter had appeared at my side asking my requirements. I ordered a large coffee and croissant and was pleasantly surprised that he spoke excellent English and was able to give very comprehensive directions on how to get to the Giuseppe Verdi Conservatory of Music where I knew Marilyn was studying. It was situated right in the centre of Milan in Via Verdi, a street that was named after a famous composer and was considered to be one of the most important music institutions in Italy. I was not sure how I was going to find Marilyn, or what I was going to say or do, but the city was oozing with romance and I was not about to leave Marilyn at the mercy of all these self-assured handsome young Italian men, who, under the influence of a glass of vino coupled with the heat of the sun, I'm sure could be very persuasive.

I located the college after a short cab drive; the driver, who I'm sure took advantage of me, knowing that I had no concept of the value of the Italian notes I had in my pocket, had charged an outrageous amount for such a short journey. Ten thousand lire sounded such an exorbitant amount of money. As the taxi pulled up outside the school, I stepped into the street, alighting from the smallest Fiat I had ever been in, what appeared to be more like a child's toy car than a taxi. Glancing upwards at the building, I immediately acknowledged that it was very old and seeped in history. I was in complete awe of the stunning architecture that I was directly looking at.

I entered the building through large wooden doors into an impressive black and white tiled hallway with a very high ceiling, giving the illusion that I was in very grand surroundings. A very attractive English-speaking receptionist greeted me who, after looking me up and down obviously identified that I was British from my strange choice of clothes. She continuously smiled at me, laughing, every now and again glancing up at me over the top of her glasses, looking at the way I was dressed, which now seemed completely out of place in this artistic sophisticated city. After going through numerous lists she was able to tell me that Marilyn was currently in class, and after explaining my circumstances which she thought very romantic, let me wait for her in the corridor that led to the classrooms. All Italians seem to embrace romance with all their being.

And at that moment I felt very Italian.

Marilyn walked towards me her arms draped

around what looked like another young English girl student. They were singing and giggling as they made their way up the corridor. She had no idea that I was watching her. The sun had tinged her skin and brought out the tiny freckles that I used to tease her about, her hair was even blonder than before and hung in a wild unruly mass of curls around her shoulders. There was a slight redness to her skin, showing too much exposure to the Milan heat. How I loved her at that moment was beyond all comprehension. Marilyn looked up and saw me, then burst into fits of uncontrolled laughter. "Oh, Bob," she said. "What on earth are you wearing?" The moment was ruined and instead of her running straight into my arms, we both couldn't stop laughing. Over dinner in a tiny very busy cafe regularly frequented by all the music students, she told me that she thought that her course was too intense, and that her Italian tutor, although thinking she was a good singer, would never be a great one. She had written to her parents to tell them she was coming home.

So I need not have bought the Panama hat after all. I wondered if I returned it they might perhaps offer me a refund. Marilyn said, "That would be a bit of a cheek." The first thing Marilyn did the next day was take me to an Italian outfitters.

We threw away my socks and sandals, and I emerged like an Italian gigolo – cream trousers, crocodile shoes, linen shirt. I drew the line at the gold chain. I told her I'd be mugged for it back in Millwall. Marilyn laughed at me and said that I looked like an Italian stallion. I thought she sounded just like me mum. We then embarked on the most romantic two weeks of our lives. We took the train to Lake Como and dined in one of the waterside cafes, took a moonlit boat trip over the lake, drank Chianti and listened to melodious guitar music with an old Italian singing love songs that neither of us understood, then back to the boarding house for hours of passionate and urgent lovemaking.

We found a small coastal resort a stone's throw away from Milan, but we never went swimming, I had seen the gigantic sea creatures that the fisherman had caught, and they were nothing like me mum used to bring us home on a Friday night in newspaper. It was the honeymoon before the marriage, but this time I made sure that there would be no unwanted accidents to take home.

On our return, I kept a low profile for a while from Marilyn's parents. Micky said that he thought I'd gained a certain maturity from my recent holiday and my dress sense had improved considerably. I saw

Marilyn every waking, sleeping moment I could. Although on her return, she has taken a job as a music teacher in the local school so this now limited our romantic daytime trysts considerably until the school holidays.

Marilyn's parents eventually, after much persuasion, gave in to our constant requests to allow us to marry. What a wedding we had. Relatives came out of the woodwork on her side of the family, although on my side the church it seemed very empty. Although halfway through our vows I was sure I heard me mum and turning round could see her wiping a tear from her eye and could hear her say, "You're a lucky boy, Bob. You look after her."

When I told Marilyn later that evening she said, "Don't be silly. You've had too much to drink," but I still kept seeing Mum out the corner of my eye throughout the evening, winking at me and smiling. Mum was never one to miss a party. After that I failed to mention it to anyone else in case they thought I was barmy.

No expense had been spared. Marilyn's dress was purchased from a designer shop in London, after many fruitless hours of visiting bridal boutiques with her mother. I could not believe how much it had cost.

I would not have minded what she had worn, but Sally still discreetly sewed the pearl buttons onto Marilyn's dress that had been on me mum's. It was as if me mum was still here. I could hear her saying, "You've done so well for yourself, Bob." Charlene was bridesmaid along with Marilyn's younger cousin Amanda. How we kept her in a dress for that long I will never know. Charlene looked more like Sid every day. She had the most amazing sense of humour, and as wild as she was, we would always laugh with her, not at her, because she was not disagreeable like her father had been.

Uncle Jimmy was just about still alive but very elderly. He insisted on being my best man, although due to his rheumatism he could hardly stand and unfortunately fell asleep before the speeches, so my friend Mickey Ash had to take over.

Marilyn looked like a vision as she walked towards me down the aisle, and when the vicar pronounced us man and wife I felt my heart would burst. We didn't have a honeymoon. We put the money towards the house that we had recently purchased in Lewisham. It wasn't as posh as Marilyn would have liked but I wanted to do it on my own and not be beholden to her parents.

I always promised her I'd take her back to Milan one day, to recreate those romantic memories we had. It was to be a long time coming, however. A year to the day, Bert, my first boy, was born, and as he was put into my arms by the doctor that snowy winter's night I remembered Garndiffaith. So, holding this tiny bundle upwards to heaven, I presented him proudly to me mum and dad, and looking into his sleepy half-open blue eyes, I promised my son in that moment that as long as there was breath in my body he would never have to wear cardboard in his boots.

The End

Printed in Great Britain
by Amazon